THE BURIAL AND
OTHER SHORT PROSE,
1963–1994

CARAF Books

•

Caribbean and African Literature
Translated from French

<small>RENÉE LARRIER AND MILDRED MORTIMER,</small> *Editors*

THE BURIAL AND OTHER SHORT PROSE, 1963–1994

MOHAMMED KHAÏR-EDDINE

COMPILED AND EDITED BY **ABDELLATIF ABBOUBI**

Translated by **Conor Bracken**

UNIVERSITY OF VIRGINIA PRESS
Charlottesville and London

The University of Virginia Press is situated on the traditional lands of the Monacan Nation, and the Commonwealth of Virginia was and is home to many other Indigenous people. We pay our respect to all of them, past and present. We also honor the enslaved African and African American people who built the University of Virginia, and we recognize their descendants. We commit to fostering voices from these communities through our publications and to deepening our collective understanding of their histories and contributions.

Originally published in French as *L'enterrement et autres proses brèves, 1963–1994*, compiled and edited by Abdellatif Abboubi
© 2009, William Blake & Co.

University of Virginia Press
This translation and edition, with afterword, glossary, and bibliography
© 2026 by the Rector and Visitors of the University of Virginia
All rights reserved
Printed in the United States of America on acid-free paper

First published 2026

9 8 7 6 5 4 3 2 1

ISBN 978-0-8139-5470-7 (hardback)
ISBN 978-0-8139-5471-4 (paperback)
ISBN 978-0-8139-5472-1 (ebook)

Library of Congress Cataloging-in-Publication Data is available for this title.

Cover design: Joel W. Coggins

CONTENTS

THE BURIAL AND OTHER SHORT PROSE, 1963-1994

THE BURIAL

At the moment, snow is shedding dark blotches of earth, and a child is playing in it. He ran away from his house a while ago and can't remember a thing about it right now. He was in a whole new world, one that someone once described to him, albeit vaguely. It's like everything began and ended there; as he ponders the snow patch, the child senses the presence, somewhere, of living beings. But his memory is useless, truncated. He feels a vague urge, a sensation that might not be warm, but is at least reassuring. Sometimes he looks at his feet, other times at the horizon. He doesn't understand anything about this blank speechlessness accenting his solitude. Something, though, trembles in his throat, and in the deepest recess of his flesh, an almost palpable tenderness takes shape.

The child runs off, yelling, gibbering. Then stops—he feels a sharp circle tighten around him as everything takes on a new shape. He shakes himself, like he's trying to shed some thick, heavy crust that had been paralyzing him. This is when he sees a keyhole of light that every now and then some shadows disrupt.

The child shivers and then collapses. Standing back up, he inspects the spot of light and approaches it cautiously. He opens his eyes again and rubs them. His mother is holding him in her arms. Two women are sitting on the other side of the room. The younger one is weeping. A man with grizzled hair paces around. He seems worried and doesn't look at the child smiling at him.

"He's going to get better," his mother says. Then, after a brief silence, she says, "The doctor was right." The two women look at the child. The weeping one sniffs and tidies her disheveled hair. The man sits down on a sheepskin. His hard, hollow features give his face a haunted look. He mutters, but no one is listening; he's more skeptical about the child's health. He'd been through things like this, like when he was brought at a very young age to the home of close family friends, people who were so kind he preferred them to his own parents. Ever since, he's always been scared of these situations. Life doesn't come back—if it leaves once, it leaves forever. Your son's smile tells me many things.

His aunt was lying down on her cot. She was speaking, but her face shone with something terrible, like a black monster was stroking her heart.

She isn't going to die, the *fquih* had said, the *fquih* who was so close to God. But he was wrong. Death comes from illness, not the sky. It had immobilized my aunt after it made her say what she didn't want to say. I'm not tired anymore. I'm no longer in pain. Go on, everyone, leave, get out of here. But you, my son, stay . . . And then she was dead by evening, while the cool dark in the trees smothered, farther off, the cicadas' singing. She gave a little jerk and then went still, her eyes fixed on the ceiling. Eyes full of a thin blueness! The child thought she had gone to sleep so that the women would leave. What a good aunt she was! A day or so earlier, she'd talked to him again about a trip to the mountains he'd been excited about. You want a hare, it's yours. You want a partridge, you'll have it. She'll wake up before dawn and we will set off without anybody knowing. We'll catch ourselves a hare. I'm a really good runner, right auntie, he murmured in her ear. I'll catch it before we get back to the village, I'll cut its throat and we'll eat it together, just us two. And then I'll tan its skin for my drum. You can come with me to the stream, I'm going to need some laurel wood.

These recollections, sizzling like lightning, sliced through his memory like a sharp knife through a lamb's throat, but instead of hot blood, out leapt silhouettes that evaporated immediately, leaving only a crisp idea. I said your son isn't going to pull out of it, the man said again. The mother looked at him with pity and shrugged. He has these ideas sometimes . . . they say he's crazy. She went back to rocking her child as if nothing had happened. But the man's words broke over her entire body, splintering into needles that stuck in her gut and irked it. The child was no longer smiling. He stared at the man almost in shock. He looked like he was saying "You want me dead, whatever the cost; I thought you loved me. You're lying—I'm not going to die!" However, the man clearly sensed death and thought that it was going to make the child say, as it had his aunt before, what he didn't want to say.

The women noticed me. They yelled, "Your aunt is dead, yet you're talking to her." I said she was just sleeping. I didn't want to let on what we were planning on doing. The ruse worked, my aunt's sleep. I leaned back over to her again and told her nobody had a clue about our upcoming adventure. But the women were still there. The older one recited prayers all while keeping an eye on me; the more she kept at it, the less I cared. My mother was crying in a corner; she wiped her nose with part of her *haïk*.

The woman sits on an old stool. The child has closed his eyes. His face is pale again. Sweat runs down it in long rills, falling in droplets on his mother's dress.

The snow! Now the snow is an ashy color. Out of it jut roofs around which a wind thick with dust and pebbles bucks and twists, then falls on itself in a violent contortion. The child gropes around hopelessly among the upheaval. The wind pushes him back every time he tries to get close to a roof and wallops him over and over in the face and the chest and the stomach. The child grows numb. It feels like tiny creatures are chewing on him so he'll give up trying to tear off this roof—so close!— and plunge inside into the house below, where, no doubt, things will be more peaceful.

He's shaking again, the mother says. I'm worried this old fool might be right.

The old woman had told mama to call the *fquih,* but she didn't dare. So the old woman went herself. When she came back, he was with her. He looked at my aunt a long time and said, "Make sure that everything is ready. I'll go notify the *moudden* so he can announce her death tomorrow morning." As he was going to leave, I grabbed his arm and asked him what they were planning to do with my aunt. He replied that she was dead and that she would be buried tomorrow, but I didn't believe him. I wanted to tell him about our adventure. I would have, too, if my aunt hadn't been right there. The old woman almost slapped me. I ducked, heard my aunt's voice.

And then I was back. It was an owl's cry. It had perched on the terrace wall. He had two huge eyes. As soon as I saw him, I staggered. He stayed stock-still. Deep in his glassy pupils strange scenes played out. I wanted to sneak up and grab him so I could give him to my aunt, but the old woman grabbed me. This time she smacked me. I insulted her. My mother stood up and held me to her and apologized for my behavior. Then she made me sit on her lap . . .

The child manages to grab onto the foliage of a half-buried tree. He can't feel his heart beating anymore. His head is heavy and feels on fire. A cough sticks in his throat. A sudden jet of water in his stomach—he curls up for a moment before a long and painful stream comes out of his mouth. He's vomiting, the mother says. That must be doing him some good.

The man glances at them quickly and grimaces. She wipes her arms clean and tells one of the women to clean the floor.

When I woke up, the sun had just barely risen. I tiptoed over to the place where my aunt had been the day before, but she was no longer there. So I decided to search the house. A harsh smell pleated the air. On the ground floor I found the women. I asked them where my aunt was and they said with God. I didn't understand what they meant so I asked again. Eventually, they said one day I'd understand. I left, unhappy. I thought my aunt had betrayed me. She didn't want me to come along with her, even though she knew that I was strong and knew how to hunt. I thought about it as I walked. Once I got to the edge of the village, I saw far off some men dressed in white and I started to run. I fell several times; my hands and knees bled. The men gesticulated a lot with their hands . . .

He's not eating anything anymore. It's been two days and two nights and he's vomited up everything we give him. And he isn't sleeping. He's constantly shaking. We have to call the doctor again, the mother says. The man waves his hand in front of the boy's eyes, as if to shoo a fly, then scratches his chin, his neck . . .

I was lying behind a pile of oblong rocks. In the crown of a palm tree crows croaked. Something, like a kind of swarm, rose up my legs. I couldn't stop rubbing them. The men were sitting in rows. They recited verses. I thought I could hear words I'd learned in the mosque. Their voices pierced the sky and fell back down, spreading along the stony ground. It wasn't possible for me to dream at that moment, but I imagined I might be able to pick my way among them and pass somehow undetected. Beyond them, a man was digging. Another was cutting branches off a jujube tree and putting them into a pile. I burned to join them but something held me back and blurry shadows reared up each time I tried.

Then, out of nowhere, a pinhole of shadow! A bottomless night, and all around and everywhere else an intense luminosity. Maybe that's the way. The child already wants to step into the hole. But as soon as he tries to stand up, he falls down and hurts himself. Out of this shadowy hole a coolness wafts, covering him in caresses, but the day's mallet continues to pound burning rings onto his forehead that ripple through his head and slam into his soul. He thinks it might be better to burrow in without stopping. Then this brightness would stop harassing him. But what about this path, so calm and so close? Maybe it leads to a kind of final peace. If he were to follow it, he'd no longer be a prisoner of this pain-stricken body that haunts him, nor of this cold and heavy earth that is smothering him, itching for the moment it can enclose him and get to grinding him apart.

A small old man stood up. He signaled to the man digging to stop, then all the others stood up. I didn't know what they were doing and that bothered me. Was something bad going on? Why all these men? And who was this small old man? The more I wondered, the more fear filled me up. Fear? No, it was something else. I was as mute and immobile as one of those oblong rocks. Suddenly, I remembered my aunt. A bolt tore through my heart. Blood scorched, I leapt out of my hiding place and ran up to the old man. It was the *fquih!* I yelled and veered toward the hole already filled up with dirt. A man grabbed my arm and shook me so hard tears sprang up in my eyes. Some of them asked me who I was, but because I didn't want to say anything, others gave my name. I yelled that it was just me and my mother and I don't remember ever having a father. They reddened and mumbled. That's all it took for the *fquih* to decide I was crazy and needed a little discipline. What a liar! I hated crazies. I shook violently but recovered quickly, like a cat after a big leap, thinking I might tear off his spotless djellaba. The man who grabbed my arm could barely keep hold of me. They all spat in my face, except for the man holding me; he slapped me and threw me to the ground. Later on, I learned he'd been in prison several times due to his antisocial behavior and that our people for a long time had avoided him like a sickness. Once I got back up, I ran home crying. Same thing there! Had someone warned them? My mother boxed my ears. All the little girls burst out laughing. I laid a couple of them out, I don't really remember, and then I ran off to hide in the stables. It stank but at least it was safe. My feet sank in the manure. Just like in the mud, I remembered, one time after the stream had subsided a little (that day, it'd carried off some kid that they'd ended up being able to rescue; his mother called everyone to help . . .). The cow licked my hands. I rubbed her rump, right above the pink-white button under her tail, caked in dried shit. It was moving, I mean it was pulsing—I knew what it was. The urges were already coming at me then from everywhere. It seemed like some overwhelming game in which you both died, one inside the other, but you didn't disappear, because the body was where it all started. Like everything else, like the life of men, it wasn't all that serious, but then there was this water filling up my mouth—as soon as I swallowed it, there it was again. It was like this every time: I decided to take care of something, and then something else crashed into me and worried me. It was never as if there was only ever a single thought in my head, as the saying goes, but it's not the same thing at all—it always seized me from outside. And then, as I was tapping the cow's "strawberry button"—my granddad called it that; whenever he called it that I couldn't take it—I drew back as if singed, because I thought I heard someone hiding in the back, in the darkness. In fact I'd heard some small sounds: a breath, someone sniffling, maybe; this had definitely happened before in a dream, when I still had a granddad. I'd leapt a hedge, was in a guardhouse where I played a lot with a friend; but this time, it wasn't a dream, I was there, stuck in a corner while the cow chewed its slow cud. Gradually, I realized I was stuck in the mud; I felt like I was tangled in some huge net beside a stream. I yelled for help but only I could hear my voice. Awful tremors wracked me. And then I hushed, like someone looking for a way out, like a rat trapped and hurt who quits whining for a second. These silent minutes were useless, but not entirely; pitying oneself doesn't mean anything; you need to feel smooth, spread evenly everywhere, as big as the world—that's how I liked to feel. But it didn't last long—my entire being left me, traveling through the manure, the odors, the rustling of the many sudden hands of my enemy lying in wait, surrounding me on every side. Besides this faint whistling and the occasional flex of a wing that sometimes blinded me, nothing else reached me. My face hurt, my eyes in particular. This cruel image (it's as clear as if it were in a mirror) drained the color from my cheeks so they looked like a rotting watermelon or week-old dung: between two boulders was a passage like a hallway, steep on the other side; you have to climb up because it leads to the mountain; flies everywhere, and toads, too, the day after rain; worms wriggled around, fat and white, pointy at both ends, and they twisted around when kids prodded the heap of them; they'd put them in the sun to watch them writhe; it was entertaining . . . Fuzzy insects buzzed in the dark; they stuck to my skin; I brushed them off, sometimes covering my head with my hands. The struggle wasn't going to end as soon as I'd thought, though—maybe the guy was the reason for this, I told myself. In any case, it was fatal, it had the feel of something premeditated. He launched his microbial tempest at me in long gusts, to make it easier to capture me, no doubt . . .

The child is sinking in a muddy pond where the sun has ceased to be itself. His body is white-hot. The cracked sky falls in uneven heavy shards. Under the water there are chambers. They seem to have been built by crabs or fanged amphibians. The mountains that had once been there have collapsed in such a way that only shattered rocks remain. The bottom is like a deck of anthracite stars. This world seems vertiginous. The child feels a profound solitude again, but he's barely suffering; his entire body is a burn; he doesn't feel it, the feeling can't root. His skin is as hard as the shell of a turtle. Then he stops, grabs onto some obstacle, a stony handle or a branch jutting out at random, and he inspects his limbs for a while before letting the stone or branch go and falling down again, heavy as he is . . .

And finally, he's out of it! He was everywhere and I couldn't see him. He wouldn't let me move. I could see so easily the cracked door. The day's beams passed through it. They snapped

off sometimes but not for more than a second. I imagined someone behind the door. They might have been able to save me
but I couldn't yell, I couldn't even gesture faintly. It was like
I was caught in a fog gone solid. I could distinctly hear the
voices of women and children. They were looking for someone.
Tirelessly. Me, for sure. He was weighing down my heart, my
stomach, my lips. I was done for; I managed to jump a little.
Eventually, I realized my resistance was useless and I'd have
to let myself get caught; I ground my teeth to cracking. I was
stuck, just like my adversary. That's why no doubt he escaped
by tearing himself to pieces, but I saw him—he was a mobile
flame. Later, once I'd told my mother what had happened the
day they buried my aunt, she forbade me from leaving the
house. Obviously, I didn't listen. I needed to tell everyone, especially the kids who thought they were stronger than me, that
I was a hero. Alas! I wasn't able. I was crushed. My mother had
to bring me to see an old healer who lived in another village. If
I remember right, we walked all morning; we'd gone the wrong
way. This is how, though, I finally found the mountain. It was
just like I'd imagined it; that someday I'd go beyond my house,
that I'd walk among enormous boulders, that strewn everywhere there'd be spiny trees and plants that were only green
in summer, that I'd hear the strange cries that were probably
animals hidden in their lairs. I saw a jackal; it looked at me; it
ran, then turned back, stopped now and then, immobile as it
stretched out its paws. I saw particolored lizards, translucent
and delicate snakeskins; some people said they helped with certain sicknesses. I rubbed them against my stomach and chest.
My mother pointed out to me the place where some years ago
a thief had robbed a traveling young woman of her jewelry.
She must have been traveling alone. I shook with anger. I knew
I was weak—everyone told me so; it was an effective insult; I
considered it a failure I was responsible for. But I was still able
to beat up all the other kids; I was the scourge of the village.
One winter morning, when they'd just slaughtered two bulls
(I forget the name of the holiday), I was playing with one of
the bladders tossed away by the butchers when the son of one
of the butchers came at me fast. I kept on inflating the blad-
der but he wouldn't go away. Gradually, other kids made a

ring around us; they goaded me on, yelling that I was too limp to beat the butcher's son because he ate more meat than me and that I wouldn't dare cross him. I knew I could bring him down, though. Something held me back for a second and then I grabbed him by the throat and brought him down. I sat on him. He was at my mercy. I was furious; shame gnawed at me and I whaled on his face relentlessly. His cheeks and lips were bleeding. The other kids crowed with joy—this was their favorite kind of show. Once I felt a little tired, I leapt up, to everyone's surprise, and with heavy steps I managed to flee for home. The butcher caught me as soon as I put my hand on the door and gave me a thrashing before throwing me scornfully against the wall. I wasn't able to cry. Only once I was inside did the tears come. My mother had me drink a bowl of whey and tried to console me. She promised me she'd have it out with the wife of my tormentor. She said it was unfair for adults to get involved in kids' squabbles. While I sniffled, she talked, pacing the room. Now and then, she'd stop to wipe my face. I was innocent. Didn't I know it! Weird feelings took shape inside me. Something scampered around on top of my heart. I started to cry again. This time, I sobbed. Then she took me in her arms, saying how heavy I was, to help me forget the whole thing. This was her way of showing me I wasn't alone, that she'd never abandon me, whatever came to pass. Once, I'd demanded that she direct all her affection toward me. Just before my younger brother came into the world, she had to wean me off her milk. She gave me instead the solid foods I was getting used to. But I refused them: I was too attached to her breasts. Imagine—at five years old I was still breastfeeding. It had to change. The whole family, and a neighbor, too, got together to strategize. They tried to convince me I'd grown to be such a big boy that I had to give up bad habits. That didn't work. I swore I wouldn't eat a single thing. My mother, soft-hearted, indulged me, and they all tore into her for this, vigorously. It was only much later that she succeeded in putting me off her milk and onto the joys of dishes like couscous with butter and meat. I took to this new habit so well that all I wanted to eat was meat. An aunt would bring it to me every time there was a village holiday. Now, I loved food, myself, and being right.

I'm fine, mama, he says, rubbing his eyes. What happened to me? Where am I? It seems like it isn't him speaking. That's strange, the old man thinks. He's started to talk again. The young woman hides her face. They're inside me, she says. Then, nothing else. She tears at her hair, opens her mouth wide, howls without a sound. Then she leaps up, takes a few steps and keels over heavily, arms and legs spread, a line of spittle in the corner of her lips. Get up, the old man yells at the other woman, and get some water and onions. Bah—this house! The elders can't keep themselves in check. The other woman doesn't move, still dumbstruck. So the old man goes to find water and onions. When he returns, he leans over the young woman, opens her mouth, and pours a little water in, which she spits up. He takes out a penknife, quarters the onion, takes the smallest piece and rubs it on the young woman's cheeks. He mutters, visibly angry. Get up and help me. The old woman doesn't move. The mother is sitting on a chair, child in her arms; she seems to be enjoying the show. The old man slaps the young woman three times. Nothing doing! She grunts and drools. I'm wasting my time, he thinks; he stands up, frozen in place for a moment before leaving. He goes into another room and throws himself onto an unmade bed and starts cackling. Here's how it goes—the song and dance were basically done by the time she lost consciousness. They brought her to her house immediately and called the *fquih*, who spent all night at her bedside. The following day, she was herself again. The demon's enemy is the spirit—a weak spirit invents it and a strong spirit destroys it. He gets up, satisfied, returns to the room, clears his throat, and begins to read a verse aloud. At the same time, he sees the woman in his imagination. What are you doing? the mother asks. The old man doesn't reply. The young woman groans, turns over, fists clenched. Her face is no longer visible. At the moment, she is crying, like a child . . .

ASINUS, ASNOUS, AND ASS

Writing in French is an intentional choice that wasn't forced on me in any way. I studied Arabic at the same time I studied French. My mother tongue, if you can call it a tongue, is Berber, though more precisely it's Chleuh (Tashlhiyt), the dialect used exclusively by inhabitants of southern Morocco. I suppose that way back when, Berber was a language shared and spoken by the ancestors of tribes whose languages nowadays differ significantly. You can even find some traces of it in Upper Egypt. But History contributed enormously in changing the underlying structures.

It struck me when I was reading *The Golden Ass* of Apuleius that the word "ass" (*âne*) is derived from the Latin *asinus*. In Chleuh, a young donkey is called an *asnous*. Where's the difference?

In the interpretation of languages, their peculiar feeding into and out of one another, it's important to believe that they arise not only out of accidents of History; there is something like a phylogenetic curiosity in humanity that compels it, like an animal, to explore its memory, thanks in part to the fact that the behavior of others, with their disparate languages and divergent dialects, is just one of multiple rays of it, a mirror held up to its slow, murky apprenticeship to life.

In the Maghreb, writing in French is virtually the same thing as writing in Arabic, due to the fact that these two languages are understood only by exclusive, often antagonistic, elites. The spoken language of the Maghreb (and I don't mean the rural language, I mean the urban one) is a dialect of Arabic that has nothing to do with literary Arabic. As long as it's like this, there can be no truly popular literature in the Maghreb. This situation is intimately linked with political progress, to the liberation or the demolition of Maghrebi peoples.

For me, I see the French language as a tool for work and an instrument for personal enjoyment. When I write, I want to reach perfection, and if what I produce doesn't thrill me, I consider it unworthy of my eventual readers. I never write for this individual, that political party, or this particular group of humans—I write for those who know how to read me and who find a little of themselves in my work. First, there is language; then there's whatever you put into it. There's the burst that cannot capture you, and that you cannot capture, unless you've mastered some word transmitted this way for a long time. That's how it is for all languages and all writers.

The attitude of certain Maghrebi authors toward the French language is an attitude of mutilated men. It's a grave mistake, since we know a writer is outside language: he is only a manifestation of History. The true writer is always a stranger in the language he expresses himself in.

There will be fewer and fewer Maghrebi writers writing in French, considering the messy, intense Arabization that is popular right now in the Maghreb. Out of this pandemonium some minor poets will probably emerge, but no true creators. These will only be some exercises in style without amplitude, and that's it! I'm not a pessimist, but the choice of language is an individual affair. One loves the words of this or that language or one doesn't. It's like food. And this is all happening right at the very moment we're beginning to open up to the world—when we are still pure, I mean. I'll go further and say that a writer does not possess a given language. It's the language that possesses him. He is actually its slave. He must accept it completely, beyond nationalities, and consider himself a writer unattached.

For me, French culture is French life as it's led day by day; it's the magnificence of the French language when one knows how to wield it; it's the encounter of men and women and the sudden occurrence of places while randomly wandering. Certain French and foreign writers have injected fresh air into this language at full boil. This is the landscape I aim to be a part of, most likely. Why should I complain about this culture? Why reproach this language that serves me so well, with its miscellaneous crevices, or the detours of men who are supposed to give it a truly human inflection but who are only playing God?

French culture, like other cultures, follows the worldly line laid out for it by History. The men who produce it should not dismiss external inputs, because if they incorporate them well and understand them well, the culture of the entire world will end up one day the richer for it.

SAVING THE FISH

This kid, this smooth-cheeked teen whom I see running through the puddles of this low mountain stream again, shoving sand around and reorganizing rocks; this kid armed with a hemp sack he holds open in front of the holes where the trout are hiding, and who, with his friends, constructs small channels with round, gleaming stones; this snot-nose is me. At a young age I discovered the joys of fishing where I'm from in southern Morocco. In summer, the stream would dry up and the fish would take refuge in holes that would eventually dry up, too, with the sun beating down on them and the earth cracking into craze-edged plates. Sometimes, I'd be digging through the sand, pulling up rocks, and discovering silver-colored fish, a kind of eel that, if I wasn't quick enough, would disappear immediately. This frantic pursuit was merely a game for me, because I never ate my prey—I'd release all the fish and turtles, especially the trionyxes, into one of our wells; I'd often cover long distances in order to satisfy this veneration of life that has always consumed me. I wanted to save the fish, not eat them. And anyway, in southern Morocco we eat lots of fish already, albeit smoked, and from the ocean. It has a wonderful flavor, one so strong I remember it easily even now; maybe this is why I've gravitated toward fishing in the sea? Who can say? What I did as a teenager acted as a kind of initiation into the art of real fishing, the kind of fishing that I began to do later, much later, and that has given me so much pleasure and even texts. Yes, texts; you might even call them poems. Fishing, like hunting, is one of the residues of those instincts we all once had but that we have refined so much they've become pleasures, a way to commune with the primordial elements and the beings who live within and are entirely of them.

Becoming a maritime fisherman overnight is difficult, and not possible for everyone. When you love the sea, you respect it. You defend its health, throw nothing into it that might harm it, because, let's not forget, oceans are the lungs of the globe, lungs, and also its breadbasket. A true fisherman, like a true farmer, must love the earth and the waters that surround us, that carry us and that are our source. A true fisherman, like a true farmer, must constantly look after his equipment. You need to grease the reel every time you're done fishing! You need to wipe the poles clean! Because this reel and this pole, the line and the hooks that procure for you so many almost unspeakable joys, are extremely fragile. It always seemed like I was somewhere high in the sky when, with a sudden shake, a fish, bream or perch, a moray or conger, shook my line, shaking me with a fierce energy as if suddenly the whole ocean surged at me with its snaps and fears and jolts that my body gripped like a calving poem. And so I reel, having first set the hook, and I fight, toe to toe, inch by inch, the fish and I'll get it, I'll yank it from the swell, the depthless, darkened swell we still don't know well despite our frogmen (a frog, you say. Could a frog really dive that deep in the sea? No, no, my friend, sorry, not possible), I'll get the fish, but not yet! Not just yet. Stay calm. And what do we have here—a bream! No, a moray! A moray? Good lord, watch out, that thing could put you in the hospital, watch out, you idiot! I fight the fish, I pull and pull and pull—ah! I don't want the line to snap, if it doesn't snap I've got the fish, and I won't jump in the air like some people, I'll look at it, without any exultation; it's beautiful, it's fresh, it's good, it's big, that's what others see but me, I see the fish, its scales, its mouth, its well-formed fins, its luminescence, yes, yes, my friend, you'll end up on my plate. That's what I say to myself, while others around me and the fish hop around; suddenly transformed into a terrible, benevolent god, I am good because I am the bearer, now, of the shivers crudeness dreams of, and I am terrible because I am a killer, a purveyor of proteins wrested from the earth and the sea. How many times have people danced around me as I pulled from the heaving tide a bream or a perch, a conger or a moray? Me, a poet, a writer, at my simplest, a man.

Everyone tells themselves some kind of story while they fish. Fishing is a smoothing out, a release from the crowd, a sharp genetic memory that shows the fisherman as it shows those who watch him the fleeting images of a bygone life lost long ago, perhaps as soon as it began.

OF DJINNS AND MEN

This old angular woman scraping again at my dreams, this specter, she's nothing: just some old woman whose razor blade spangled my face with scars. This is what happens in my homeland! Right in my village, where the timeless tradition of pagan sacrifices holds sway.

In Morocco, our civilization derives from an oral written tradition. Other kinds of written tradition have come along and imposed their phenomenal vertigoes thanks to various invaders: Latin (Rome), Arab (Koran), French (current Maghrebi literature). Morocco, and the Maghreb itself, contains a component, though, that no historical contingency or external imposition can account for. For the Berbers, imps, genies, "*deofels*" are caused by the evil eye; women might miscarry and say that the sky, the moon, space (the mathematical kind) made them bleed. A man who perishes in the prime of his life is automatically the victim of the evil eye. It's understood that a woman cannot deploy the evil eye: that's science. But men can! Because a man living in this half-forgotten world eyes up day after day the women, the elderly, and the children he lives among.

In the olden days, which is to say during my childhood, here's what they'd tell us: *"You have to be Muslim! One day, when the prophet was old, death came to his house. Death knocked on the door and his slave, having seen death, told the prophet not to open it and the prophet responded: 'Go on, open it, he's come to bring me to God!'"* "Death was black and transparent, with soot-black hair." Whoever feared death saw nothing but a twist of light in front of them, squirming in the air. My childhood went off without me, while every night I, who feared no imp and who lived intensely in the sky, I went off elsewhere. In fact, I crossed the river, walked the cemetery, through the black night, seeking some prey maybe? I found the earth and the sky burned ink-black!

In Morocco several types of spirits exist: Aïcha Kendicha, Bougho, Tagmart Ismadal (mare of burials). Aïcha Kendicha and Bougho are psychic rattles people shake at night. A dissuasive function. If you don't behave yourself, Bougho and Aïcha Kendicha will gobble you up. On the other hand, Tagmart Ismadal isn't aimed at kids but at adults. She is all at once a wild mare, a flesh-eating horse like in the twelve labors of Hercules and, more scientifically, the hyena that digs up the dead. She's the one that when she's hungry pursues men lost in the dark, but is also, it goes without saying, the guilty conscience of arrogant people. An old story goes that Tagmart Ismadal was following a man all night but the man, as he grew weaker, wasn't able to outrun her anymore and so climbed the first palm tree he came upon . . . Tagmart Ismadal started attacking the tree immediately . . . and at the moment the tree was about to fall over, a rooster crowed—dawn had broken, and Tagmart Ismadal evaporated into the air. She is the equilibrium of day and night, of the stability and the landslide that the shadow offers to those who live in geological dread.

Another story: of *djins,* more well known.

A *djin* never peels itself from its man; it's an amulet, sometimes a prayer or, at its most basic, a shadow. Some people tell unbelievable stories about the power of *jnouns,* but there are no *jnouns* outside people's imaginations. In the hinterlands, little pyramids of round rocks, round stones—no schist, schist is only good for covering the dead in their graves—little pyramids, pebble by pebble, denote the place a virtuous man was killed. A cenotaph, really.

A man is returning from the souk, followed by a black dog.

Entering his house, he says:

"I was followed by this black dog."

But the black dog retorts:

"What are you talking about, I'm a *djin.* Sure I followed you, it's because I couldn't feel safer than in your house, but if you rat me out, misery will tan your hide!"

The man, this *djin,* these imps, this evil eye, have they not all sprung from the sprained imaginations of men who just want to go somewhere, anywhere else?

In the Moroccan south, each night a shard of the heavens scatters these and other terrors, other joys.

RETURNING TO MOROCCO

Here we are, finally at home, I say to myself often. And? Two years now, and what's it add up to? "We aren't bankers or shopkeepers, adding things up," a little voice squeaks out of the abyss inside me, the same voice that arranged and syncopated books like *Résurrection des fleurs sauvages, Agadir,* or *Le déterreur* . . . This little voice that surfaces from the bottom of my childhood yet knows how to keep a record of doubts and failures without ever falling into despair despite the shocks and uncertainties, the tribulations of all stripes. And what have you gained from this sudden return, undertaken no doubt on a whim? No castle or spot in the limelight, as far as I know, but there is the freedom to roam again those spotless solitudes that have always nourished my work, without which the work wouldn't be what it is, with its turbulent shading characteristic of the world's beginning. And yes, I've at least gained from it a serene maturity, as well as the rich stream of fresh images able to make texts shimmer. If I hadn't come back, sooner or later I'd have gone through a phase shift, a serious rupture, though I wouldn't have entirely dried up as a writer. The agony would have been too great for it to happen any other way. I would have had to remove any direct reference to my homeland, not in order to forbid exoticism, a habit into which many of our defectors fell a long time ago, but more so to install myself deeper within the progressively foggier convolutions that represent the schematic development of man. And at the same time I would have had to clarify the other face of the void, the one that all beings bear within themselves: the hearth of every mystery, of life and of death. Long exploited by churches, sects of every stripe, bands of spellcasters, totalitarian States, the Spirit itself that fears going backwards even when it's to better assess one's options . . . But that creature dwelling in its shameful hollows, it's totally normal for the Spirit to shove it back into the dreariest, dankest cave in order to allow itself a clear conscience and no disturbance whatsoever, even from memory. It must constantly devote itself to erasing it, knowing that it's impossible to excise it entirely from itself, to rid itself of it, because they're indissociable, linked together, but it's not a question here of some ordinary alloy, nor a tangle of threads of different materials—it's more a question of a harmonious mixture whose harmony itself is a dissonance, a wrong tone in the universal chord.

And so I came back, to my risks and perils, to my very own land of marvels, still quite young and like so many other Third World nations struggling in some fashion under the gaze of the jockeying scavengers, and that harbors scavengers, who are much cleverer and quicker than external enemies: bad faith as an institution, hypocrisy as a badge of honorability, ignorance of daily realities, a complete lack of organization, the absence of any initiative, the frantic hunt for money one never gets, for "clandestine pleasures," for futilities and trinkets. Subterfuge, seeming in place of being . . .

This is a little bit of what I've noticed in the past couple of years. But in contrast to those crimes, to the inability to truly fulfill oneself, there is the grand generosity that is the preserve of the people and those for whom any benefit gained from a single second of community suffering is out of the question. There are also those who contemplate the balance of society, those who are nearing tomorrow's truths every day and driving far from the cloaca where stupid and stupefying minds would confine us. There is, then, or at least one must hope there is, a chance of regeneration, of attaining again the values described and lived by our ancestors, because to amount to nothing in this world means simply to fall right back into slavery or to perish from resignation or shame all while feeding yourself horsefeathers. Self-respect is first off respect for one's own land, one's ancestral memory, of all of one's values that don't ossify into clownish traditions but that develop ineluctably and parallel to the development of the species' cultural memory. This is why we refuse to wall ourselves up in ghettos or preserves or on the margins of life's growth—and why we always say "No!" to the animality that would flatten us into its own fantasies, restrain us like zoo animals annihilated by their nauseating excrement, their impotent attacks and their immoderate ugliness. In this public locker room, one is only one step from leaping the railing and finding oneself on the other side of monstrosity, where one can observe straightaway the perfection of beings and things. To find oneself wholesome, laundered in a way, sterilized and clean enough now to undertake a new task—that's magnificent. But there isn't any mysticism in communal life, at least not any purity—there is culture. By which I mean peace or war, in all of their senses, as much as retreat pure and simple, as was the case for many of our writers whose cries were able to be heard and continue, still, to reach us in echoes. This poses a grave problem: that of mutual comprehension, of communication. Because a country without mass communication is a country without culture and a country without culture is a country that's dying; one cannot survive indefinitely on a past culture transformed into folklore for tourists (Brittany, Corsica, the tiniest French hamlet too all have their own folklore) and tell oneself one's got culture. This means we must save our heritage. But we must also help the youth that is raising its voice to perfect its intellectual arms, to lay the foundation of a *contemporary culture* that will give the country a new dignity, its own wingspan instead of another nation's. Simply put, a personality that isn't glazed only in history—a living history that will develop through cycles of transmission. This is what we call being Moroccan.

THE *HASHSHASHINS*

For Hind

"Curse you, Hassan Ibn Al-Sabbah, and your uselessness to me in this era devoted to machines and Death; you promised me power, bliss, hope and all that went with it; at the time you were the head of a prominent cult in the Turkish mountains (maybe Mount Ararat, where Noah's Ark foundered?); you stuffed us full of prayers and Indian hemp (cannabis), you furnished us with the cold sweat of the mauve poppy, none other than that miraculous opium! You were doubtless a coruscating spirit and you wanted to be done with the grand illusions and fathomless depravity warping the world; you were so mighty that empires trembled at the mere mention of your name; your killers were everywhere, the entire world was crawling with them; they raised your temples on the heaps of the dead; they sang your praises as they slaughtered; and so they marauded through the lowlands, the hills and plains and, beyond the seas, throughout unstable nations; they festooned Death in garlands of poppies; in those days no slave was able to say much about us (one doesn't undermine Heaven); the acrid shadows our skins were cut from reduced all other animal skins to basic biological need; none of those who walked huffing and puffing over this foul land could keep themselves together at the sight of your image; you were the wildest idea the children of Noah could ever invent; you furnished us with the weapons we needed to execute the traitors that were our brothers; stray dogs that bit you were immediately speared and any eye that looked at you askance was poked out on the double; Hassan Ibn Al-Sabbah, Father of Darkness and of Death, your brass continues to reverberate through our synapses; we cut short no small number of existences at your behest; we reduced sturdy empires to smoke and we nipped princes and revolutionaries in the bud; we haunted the poltergeist of the spasmodic and bagged the lethal intelligence of dictators; through your virtue, we crushed armies and dark police upon the savage mirror of the Sun; we consumed ourselves day and night to dismay them; knowing that the Devil was our helper because you were his master, we took action against the accidental world such that at times our intrepidness was tried, though we put things right with every victim in order to punish the inept judges; you were the only rampart and the singular mirror! Your laws, pronounced in the sumptuous silence of the mountains, among the very rocks where scuffled the beasts they said were our ancestors, your laws and your incantation set to the rhythms of central rays of quasars fascinated everyone who had never read a thing; you enchanted us; our bodies were floating in the galactic denial of cannabis—the oceans, heavy with their wonders, sand, and rocks jutting out of time's deepest wrinkle unfurled beneath our eyes as soon as you began to speak; this is how you smoke-screened the universe . . ."

I don't know why I dreamed that or even how. Any more than I know why I shot that guy I didn't know and who'd done nothing to me. He was there, that's for sure, it was a clear chance, and there you go. I told myself I had to get rid of him, that's it; I stroked the trigger on my pistol and it went off on its own—the guy fell down. I still don't know how I even ended up in that bar. The shot set everyone screaming. They jostled, shoving to get out in a huge inhuman mass. That's when I said, "Is there anything more human than a gunshot?" Even the coffee-jockeys were flat on the ground behind the bar. I went right on drinking! Like nothing at all. The guy I'd felled was lying at my feet—he wasn't saying anything anymore, no more nudging either. Nothing had happened! I finished my drink, casually, and left. The crowd that had gathered on the street outside let me through; I was like a god who didn't give a fuck about this lowly world. No one followed me. I paused for a second in front of the fish tank at a restaurant to watch the lobsters squabble and a whim hit me but I didn't follow it. The people walking by me gave me a wide berth and looked elsewhere, never turning around. I must have smelled bad: the odor of death, maybe? In any case, they acted like they didn't see me and I dawdled, stopping now and then to gawk at shopwindows and other things. I still had my hand in my pocket and couldn't stop touching the trigger of my pistol; the line out front of the movie theater evaporated when I strode up, allowing me to see more clearly inside: nothing but ass, ass, and more ass, so much for their cinema! Afterwards, I stopped in front of a lit window displaying photos of [illegible word] with starving black children. I teared up a little for those swollen bellies struck by beriberi, and in my head ten thousand crimes were detonating. If at that moment I found in my implacable path those of heads of State, whoever they might be, I'd have gunned them down, then and there. There was room for everyone inside my hatred. These little kids who you might give a lollipop to had complicit mothers and wicked fathers. They'd been reduced to less than nothing by force! Ignorance! Ignorance, this is what you get. When I was little, I fought a lot. Nobody knew who I was, though. I took out my gun and smashed the window and then walked right off. And I started thinking of my childhood—what a pack of lies! Adults lying to kids: women, men, creatures lying to the land. Everyone was corrupt, everyone was pathetic. The first lie: when they circumcised me, they said the foreskin would become a lizard. One part of me was perfect for sacrifice in savage rituals, but another part stayed behind, the one of pure crime and enchantment. In order to live, I told myself afterwards, adults need to lie to themselves and to others. To lie is to steal, so say the axioms and religions, and to steal is to kill, says the good cop who's really nothing more than a priest. With their lies, the adults were killing inside themselves what they loved the most. Their souls were no more than blunted cleats, insignificant objects. This is how I discovered they were all lousy cowards. The worst catastrophe, the most shameful treason, the bile running through them full of worse examples, this was their soul, sweet vengeance.

"You're lucky, you traitor, really lucky. Because otherwise . . ."

"Hey, if you had my .45, you'd've done the same."

Hearing this good word in my head, I walked into a restaurant off the boulevard. They seated me at the best table, but the menu didn't really speak to me, I had something else on my mind. I needed, once and for all, to settle my accounts with the world, this world crammed full of all sorts of crimes and messes. The waiters hustled up, providing such excellent service it made me nauseous. Then they asked me to write something on a piece of paper. I told them I had no pen so they dumped a heap of pens on my table. I'd never seen so many pens all at once. Which of them to choose, which one to use to write this something these ranked, obsequious waiters were asking me to. And what to write for them, I who only speak with my pistol? The waiters were bluish-green, like the mirage that awaits the parched traveler just beyond the dune.

"Bring me more pens," I told them.

They'd taken good care of me, I could say that, I'd eaten really well; but this filthy image of black children dying of hunger and swollen by the I.M.F. (International Monetary Fund), destroyer of the Third World and that you yourself built, you Stoned Assassin! Hassan Ibn Al-Sabbah, this image shattered my appetite. Why did you do that, you bastard? It shattered my appetite because you are in your grave and you're gloating about sending me here so you can laugh about our entanglements.

When the waiters had dropped their pens on my table, a shiver shook me so hard the other tables around me trembled: instead of pens, I saw revolvers. This was the moment when some lug decided to come over and talk to me.

"You the guy who popped that joe in the dive back there?"

"Huh? Forget about it!"

"So it was you?"

"If it was me I'd tell you, big guy. Now buzz off, chucklehead."

The guy followed me. He must be one of those who's always looking for death and always finding it. But how would he skedaddle without seeing my pistol's barrel?

"You got ID?"

"Here you go!"

And I gave him a good hiding. Who was he? Some cop? At this point not even a cop would have the right to ask for your ID. It's a question of moderation, of the balance of power.

"I'm just a lizard," I told him. "And an old lizard at that. Who are you?"

"I'm Death."

"You sure about that?"

"Absolutely."

"Can you prove it?"

"Of course."

"Where'd you come from?"

"That's just it—you don't know or you don't want to know that I'm coming, knowing as you already do that inside me their deaths are always being built."

"Get that weed out of here!"

"Sooner my piece than this good weed!"

"Man, get out of here."

Because I was wandering around, some hookers trailing their pimps flounced past me. The dog-faced one smiled at me; another one who had no head grabbed hold of me. So I had to gun her down. She'd lived with guys who weren't scared, guys who never flinched but whose eyes were running along the ground now like stale tears.

Here it all is. There had been back then a black woman and our women. A black woman who would bring out of her hut, for those who ordered our parents around, bad herbs and what should be called sympathetic magic, an old story wrapped in the wobbly Intelligence of Solo. That's how it was. It will be like that again until the Last Judgment. You can quote me on that!

The one who loves me, she rhymes with nothing, because she's absolutely nothing at all! She is one and many, though never herself, though never me alone, she is a devourer!

This revulsion which had never touched me while I was in Paradise was now giving me serious trouble. All the time she's lying down and all the time she's stuffing me with her troubles: her children, her husband, her ailments; she's sick all the time! Devil take her, I want nothing more to do with her!

"So, are you going to kill me?"

"Here—take your gun!"

I am out of sight out of mind, I am

the inalterable desert that curls your Night's hair with

my seal with my pail

whose teal

water will always be for you the legacy of thunder!

The masked past is coming, looming wave, quivering, imprisoned

unhelmeted

and this complicated fragrance!
past burst out of the simple detonator-killer
coming back to tell me
what I saw in the Militia flying, who I saw?
I who never saw anything, you see
Do you know all this?
who never says their name and who is Nameless?

ELEMENTARY WORD

In the beginning, everything looked almost beautiful: I was basically swimming in light, crossing billions of particles across an endless expanse. My vigor and speed outstripped actual rays of light. In the beginning, there was nothing, but everything was like a flash, an unchanging plasma: the Big Bang maybe? They say that because everything has to start somewhere, that's just how it is. But I'm saying the Big Bang wasn't the beginning. Something truly elementary doesn't concern itself with these kinds of questions; it just is, that's it. This isn't forbidden, but it isn't moral. Moral? What's that? For something elementary, there's no philosophy, or at least not at the very beginning: that comes after. A primary element isn't a quark, nor is it a wave or an electromagnetically charged system; it's an immaterial being worth all of the light and all of the darkness of the world. A divine sight, no doubt. And anyway, I wandered a long time before settling down in a single spot. There was only a gaseous fire everywhere. And then, suddenly, everything condensed, then separated, and reconstituted itself differently. One galaxy here, another one over here, and so on. And at the center of each, autonomous gravitational zones, and far from them, the Earth, little planet that I cherish over all the rest; that's why I'm here for the duration. Though it's not so much the planet but those who live on it, not animals but humans, those weak creatures, dense and wily in bodies where I luxuriate and take my vacations, these little ingenious workshops that I manipulate as I please and in which I hatch inane dreams and apocalyptic dramas. I don't hurt these meager beings; I just amuse myself with them. Sometimes, I nestle into one of their neurons and tickle the dendrites *a piano* or *fortissimo,* all depending on my luminosity. When the vessel is too weak, it cracks; when it has a solid psyche, it froths like an ocean, and when it is calm and sure of itself, it falls right to its knees, believing it has seen in the sky its entire reason for being, and it pens its destiny on it. All mythologies are familiar with me. The fairy tales have made a big deal of my existence. The scribes have ascribed me incomparable virtues—they adored me most. But the epigones literally psychologized me, I who simply am. I have no mother or father, no posterity, I am, and that's it. I was in the scribes' good books, and the Himalayan lamas' too. Zoroaster invoked me. Job, circled by worms and reduced to nothing, called on me in his paroxysmic agony. The halos over the goddesses of every pantheon flickered on upon seeing me. Angels themselves, the kind no one makes anymore, reveled in a single sighting of me; I treated them like oafs and moved on, moved on to live a couple of instants in the enormity of a single human neuron. It's been said of me that I unhinge; that I shake up the meninges' proper organization; that I am a disturber, an obstacle to dancing in circles; that my specificity burns or nullifies the *sapiens'* codes; that this keeps the gentleman from reflection; that I am a kind of devil, though not *the* Devil; that crimes are committed at my encouragement; that one must let the machine function on its own (that's what it's been calibrated for); that to purge me, as the psychoanalysts and shamans recommend (the only difference between them being that the shamans are more poetic), one must use talismans and antipsychotics. What a farce! Given the choice I'd take a good talisman over a pill any day, even if the latter remade the Universe. Light therapy well conducted is worth a thousand sniveling chemos. The story of a man is measured by his relationships, and yes, the story of Babel is truly pitiful. Babel! People came down from the mountain and tried to raise to the sky a taller mountain, but their structure crumbled. Originally, an earthquake of extreme violence whose epicenter was their pride. I say this as the Elementary: only a handful of intellects make the world move; the rest are just bodies. I already live inside a device. I make the Void talk. Later, much later, I will reside in a plasmodic glob. And when this Earth I cherish no longer exists, I will be a static gamma, I won't change my nature; an Elementary thing exists, and that's it.

THE GHOUL

She was taller than a date palm, with legs like stilts and eyes that smoldered a demoniacal red. When she ran, sand and stones flew up around her and her frizzled hair foamed like a sea churned by a stiff breeze. Whenever she neared, the dead awoke violently but, stuck beneath the earth, couldn't flee. Every grave leaked inhuman, harrowing cries. Wild animals slunk away whenever she appeared; only nocturnal raptors, bats, and snakes didn't fear her. She bore on her body several of these creatures. She was naked, but because her skin was as armored as a rhinoceros, it wasn't noticeable. Evil spirits, the most extraordinarily infernal beings to have ever been sighted, accompanied her on her rambles. She lived in a desolate area on the edge of the desert, in a rough, stony place that the sun had blackened like a hunk of jet. Nothing grew there, but in looking closely at the contours of the terrain you could see that there had once been some kind of earthly paradise there, a tranquil, happy Eden. No traveler, even lost ones, ever chanced upon her cursed environs. Everyone knew she didn't go after the living, but her fearsome power and her paralyzing gaze made even the bravest cower.

In the nearby villages, deep in the most far-flung oases and inside the tents of nomads, people met frequently to try to seal her fate. You only needed, they believed, to find some good rifles and off her in an ambush. They'd even gotten so far as to attempt it but, every time, the riflemen threw down their weapons and took to their heels. They also went to the best *"tolbas,"* well-regarded shamans, to find out if she was a woman or some sort of supernatural entity so they could figure out which kind of dance or curse might neutralize her, but no *tolba* or sorcerer knew where she came from. "She is a companion of Ilbis," they said, "and she's much stronger than your talismans. There's nothing we can do against her. If you want to be rid of her,

sacrifice a pair of goats to this or that marabout. He will inter-
cede on your behalf with the Most High." Dozens of sacrifices
were made; graves were sprinkled with fresh blood; the ghoul,
since she was still being called that, kept on digging up stillborn
children and those who had died before ten. Even worse, since
all the children were dying at birth, everyone was convinced
she was responsible. Mothers didn't dare go about their business outside the house, and their husbands sequestered them
out of an abundance of caution. "Well," some thought, "this
ghoul must be nothing more than a fallen woman, possessed no
doubt by one or several demons. Look in the eyes of a woman
like this, get in real close and look, and doesn't she look like
the one we're looking for? During the day she wears the skin of
a woman, but at night, she turns into a monster." These kinds
of suspicions were everywhere; so were discord and social re-
jection. Old widows who'd never remarried were subjected to
blows and injuries. The ghoul continued to strike. In fact, she
was so active, it seemed like her appetite was endless. Every
morning, shredded bodies were discovered in little pieces. Some
thought they could detect in the burial mound enormous human footprints, while others saw the prints of an unusual hyena;
nobody could agree on what they really were. The dogs that
had been trained to hunt the ghoul would be found with their
bellies torn open and their guts hanging out. You'd be forgiven
for thinking that some incredibly ferocious beast covered in an
impenetrable shell must have taken them on in a duel as brief as
it was awful. Sometimes, some thought they heard their horrible
yelps just before the rooster crowed. Nobody dared go out and
see; the crack shots, the most skilled warriors, burrowed under
their covers, covered in sweat. Only in broad daylight would
they let their bravado swagger about. Often, their wives would
ridicule them, but they'd get slapped around in return, to put
things back in order. This got some of them abandoned. The
wives who left left everything behind them to swell the ranks of
prostitutes in the northern cities. They attributed their lousy fate
to an ancient curse that had continued to haunt women since
the dawn of time: "If the ghoul is indeed the cause of our losses
and she's a member of our sex, then at least we know a woman
will always avenge her sisters." Alone, the forsaken husbands

found their rhythm. They married young virgins and got back to siring the miscarriages the monster glutted herself on. As the woe piled on, they decided to alert the authorities, who rushed several sleuths to the area who were known for their impeccable intuition. They mixed in with the population, becoming peddlers, jugglers, and snake charmers. They skulked around the traveling souks dressed in rags exactly like the vagabonds', slept in all the cemeteries, and sniffed around the more questionable women, but they ended up withdrawing; no one saw them again. Before leaving, they drew up a report suggesting that the higher-ups relocate the affected populations. They even thought that the army might be best qualified for the task. "A search and sweep operation," they called it, but those highest up classified the document as undeserving of any serious consideration.

Things kept on like they did until, one day, lightning struck the hut of a middle-aged woman who screamed gruesomely as the celestial fire consumed her. Her ashes were gathered up and buried and the whole thing forgotten. Months went by, newborns began dying less, graves were no longer being dug up. And that was it.

A KILLER

He gauged the distance, aimed, but didn't fire. Sheltering behind a crystalline boulder, he was as alive as the thousands of
glimmers the sun struck awake across the landscape; he was,
himself, in this very instant, this gruff and durable stone as well
as this intense brightness and this rifle pointed at the bottom of
the valley and even this man he had decided to kill. That imbe-
cile who gave it no thought to swipe a few acres of land. "There
he is, Mr. Maâlem, Mr. tough nut to crack, who always had
everyone eating out of the palm of his hand; tables are turned,
now, though. I've got you in my sights and I've got a good idea
to send you packing *ad patres* with no one the wiser. That will
teach him." So that his weapon wouldn't flash in the sun, he'd
coated it in pitch; no more signs of life from it. It was as black as
the blackest night, and he liked it this way. He knew how to fire
the sweetest music in the world from it, but if he killed, it was
to set things right. Setting things right for him meant correcting
the injustices that certain tyrants had been able to commit from
within the preserve of natural justice because they'd sworn on
the Book and they were feared by the weak and the powerless.
"Or I'm taking him down because I want to test the hypothesis
about crime not paying or else my name's not Addi." He swore;
he'd sworn hundreds of times. He knew as he'd always known
that one of these days he'd send his tormentor to hell. He could
have strangled him, or slit his throat, but he preferred to take
him down with a single bullet. "Cleaner this way," he said. "And
since I wouldn't be touching him, God would have nothing to be
angry at me about. I'll have acted like an angel." He didn't know
the name of the guy he was taking aim at, only that he had to kill
him. "He tried to rob your mother. Remember when your uncle
died? He slept with his widow so he could pickpocket your mom
for her land. If you killed him? If you did this, you clever bastard,
you'd be doing the community a huge favor."

"I don't have a gun."

"But you don't need one—just strangle him. He's an old man."

"No way! No way, I need to keep it clean. I need to shoot him, like a rabbit in the grass."

"Here's some cash. Go buy a gun," the agitators said.

He took the money, roamed far afield, eventually finding his place among the shady characters of the cities you abscond to when you don't want the village to know where you are. He spent a lot of time with it in target practice in the mountains, not like a cowboy but like an executioner. After several years of wandering and bitterness he returned unnoticed, with a Remington he'd relieved a night watchman of after a brief scrap.

"You think everything's calm, old man. You know I've been gone, so you've done as you wish. Beating and thieving and ogling the wives of your children. You might even have grandkids, you schmuck. But what are you doing right now? Of course, having some tea, just like before. You'd never break that habit. You're worse than before, you think you rule this backwater. You addled old schmuck." He straightened up, steadied his aim and almost fired. "Wait! Not yet. Not the right moment. He's drinking his tea and there's a little girl serving it to him on a beautiful platter. I've never had that happen, nope—never. This little girl seems nice, but I have to kill him. There's no way we can both be alive at the same time. One of us needs to hit the ground and die! It's not even the stolen land that kills me—it's his smug look. What'll that get him? I could have easily been him, dreamed like him, been something else. As long as the world's turned, old guys like him have gone around the block and then called themselves wise. Wrong. They're warped. I need to shoot. If I don't shoot this old bastard, he'll die his natural death and enter paradise, that's what they say. Now she's serving him cakes. She's cute, this little girl, beautiful even. She's got his eyes. Never seen that before. Spitting image of him, but backwards. Dirty old man, you're mine."

Then he fired. The bullet shattered the old man's skull and the second one grazed the girl's thigh. "Got ya," he said.

[IN ALL SUBJECTIVITY]

"Take it slow," a friend says. Another one, always the contrarian, says, "Take him out, goddammit!" And he crosses himself and bows down. This life is hard, that's no mystery. An old bromide, not a hand brake, will communicate why everything's negative. I've got some true friends, stalwarts, and some unknown ones, too (as sayeth Supervielle). There's also no lack of duplicity among my friendships, serious mistakes for those who make them. We'll award them their pink slips soon. My friends (the indisputable ones) are with me whenever I do things nicely. I always do things head-on, but when I drift, they find a way to wriggle in and keep me from wandering too far off the path. Nice, right? Some practitioners of fake friendship, which is to say of hypocrisy, tell me stories about other friendships. I put "stories" in quotation marks. They hide absolutely everything from me. What would I rather they do? Who cares! And then, as you'd expect, they ransack your gray matter and even your soul. They risk everything for it. The worst of them are the ones who smile at you, revealing their werewolf chompers. We find them everywhere. We don't believe them. You can't trust them! They can thrash forever, which always makes their situation worse. The violence they visit on us can't go on without some kind of rebuttal. They think they can manipulate everything, but they're wrong. There's no science or truth to them, not even close! They use our own feelings as if they're acting on behalf of some dug-in faction in which some rebellious and vast madness has safely taken [illegible]. These false friends, their sick weakling tribe, are pathetic. They defile your mind. One scolds you for being yourself and the other's always shooting at your feet. And others say, "Obviously he's not being himself." What duplicity!

Writing about oneself is uncomfortable, but then there's the moment where an exorcism is necessary. In all my books there's something from my life, with the seconds and hours and days and months and years that make up my earthbound existence. Something new? Not at all! Nothing's really been new since the world was created. Except the shading, yes, that—the grayish-white turning gradually to black where colors woven into the unabridged blue of an incandescent eternity cross over one another. I won't say my name a single time, though. I will describe my life and I'll describe it just as an entomologist describes a beetle or how a zoologist describes a mammal and its phylogenesis.

How This Came to Be

This life, every life, is a drama. Parties and dramas unfurl within them, but never a clarity that might produce someone whose genetic programming short-circuits the reptile brain. Every life is a massacre, a bloody feast, a cold-blooded mental murder. It's stitched with white thread even when it's particolored. And this white swears by all cloth, even the clouds; each life is a unique rupture. But what, exactly, is a life? It's an assemblage of quarks, slight but rigid amino acids. DNA and RNA, there you go. A little ultrasonic battle that a macroscopic vantage simplifies into universal signs. But there are entire universes of antimatter and matter, timelines that cross and never mix, imperceptible, dazzling dimensions; formless beings that pass through your body and soul, so many there may as well be only one, and that mark you without your knowledge with the brisk breath of The Beginning. Beings without bones, without flesh, that don't think, that are thought of. They glorify you as they transform you into blotting paper on which they read your psychic deformities. Strange beings conscripted into the largest dismemberment in the world! Condemned to wander without support, mercilessly rejected! They are dark and light, bursting, and even though they've lived forever, they're continually erupting into trillions of overheated finales. In the shadow of this radio-galactic spectrum, the carbon I am born of infinitely ponders the question of the era.

[lines missing] of course. The erosion we know nothing about. You fall out of the sky suddenly; scorched aerolite; ape attempting a pantomime with random meaningless gestures; blotchy red tortoise with a beak like a macaw's; one-off may-bug; mantis and mosquito that haunt the cloacal swamp where the fringed sand thinks of and indexes the Great Loss!

As for me, I'm just an unhappy guy, poor and without stature, which you can tell from my waddling gait, hasty gestures and words and swaying. I'm moving forward, yes; I support myself, all that being said. Said against the people of my tribe. I move down a dusty road toward an ancient temple ruined by weather and vandals, along dust, billions of grains of dust that no doubt obscure the old writing that changes with each new powerful glance. I'm making my way toward a war more horrible than all the bloody news items splashed across the tabloids' front page. A calamity crammed with the world's disorder where the genes of every creature lead an infernal dance.

Inside my genes two old men continue their act, the ones who peddle my skin, who mend it, patch it up, trace on it plans without tomorrows. But they're thinking of marriage, a pact, while an unprecedented war has begun to mutilate a large swath of the planet. They walk with sure steps in the shadows of agaves, cacti, hognose snakes and lone crows; they're horseless, going on foot, and the sun shines in their eyes. They're not shuffling; they're far from the death that's raking the fields of Europe. But these old men have seen others; they too have battled [lines missing] once in the face.

The War was on. A brass-tacks one that killed not only the body but all the sense that had ever been able to reinvent us in the grand delirium in which some still lavishly exult.

Things everywhere were splitting open; what fell from the sky wasn't biblical manna but phosphor bombs!

"And what if our children married?" the first old man asks. "An alliance is better than a feud, right?"

"That could be alright. This year, the harvest is good, our livestock are fat and many and the colonist has left us in peace. He still recognizes our bravery even though we whupped him not long ago. Your daughter is pretty, healthy, hardworking . . . She'd be great for my son, who you know is a skilled horseman. He's not very educated and hasn't been to the mosque a lot, but he's loyal and brave and that's most of what makes a man. But your daughter's only twelve, and my son is fifteen."

"Age? What's that matter? They'll figure out just fine how to get along without us."

"Probably. But, tell me, the old debt—you plan to settle it?"

"Ach! You want to wade into litigious territory! Fine! If your son marries my daughter, everything will be settled. It's an alliance, pure and simple. We need to grow and protect our heritage."

The old men walk along a river, its waters murky. It has rained the night before: a storm so strong that the villagers hid out in the lowest parts of their stone homes. They lit fires that night and told each other tall tales and war stories; some prayed [lines missing] were screaming without cease, because they couldn't sleep. Dogs barked and the shocked, scrawny jackals responded to the challenge, a challenge that went back to the time when Man first tamed the dog by luring it with the leftovers of his daily hunt. The hundred-year-old cedar forest, bushy and tall, rocked to the tempest's rhythm; the wind whistled and groaned through its branches. The panther and the caracal, even the Barbary ape, abruptly went to ground. Only a few donkeys here and there brayed without fear. Which is why the river, that morning, was muddy.

There were tumuli everywhere, among the trees from which fibers dangled: votives conjuring the empire of signs of the momentous night when Being was transmuted and schematic Reason became binary: an implacable and cybernetic stridency imagined by a philosopher crawling with Sumerian ants. Photosynthesis injected tectonic carbon into this putrid mud, fashioning a light that lends the future's tide the colors of the Rainbow.

"I'll give my daughter to your son," the oldest one says.

His head was shaved and he wore a white turban mottled with flies. The other, seeing them, says:

"You've got flies on your turban, right there, in the back."

"Let them have a free ride, they need it, poor creatures. They're going to the souk, like us."

"Well, there it is—we agree. We'll marry our children. I hope they'll be happy."

The village was located on a stony promontory, not far from the old-growth forest; down below, the rolling hills became plains whose rolling charmed the eye; tufts of tough grass were allowed to live there because they'd decided to spare it, either out of fear or because the grass kept the land fertile [lines missing] some bushes that goldfinches nested in rose along the hills from which worn-down boulders jutted like spearheads; at regular intervals, scrubby thickets and small farmhouses; here, everything seemed man-sized; but, scattered around, there were tents and, grazing, sheep and cows. The exceptional calm washing over the region had no guarantor. Because it was spring, the earth was humid and multicolored flowers brightened the countryside; one could only get around by sinuous paths that ran among the fields where all varieties of vegetable flaunted their riotous flowers, where butterfly wings shimmered at the slightest breeze, a [haft?] or an animal's tail brushing a stalk.

MY GRANDMOTHER

When I look as far back as I can into the past, I see again the silhouettes of my two grandmothers, my father's mother and my mother's mother. The former was thin and dry, smart, hardworking and gentle—she got along with everyone. The latter, already on the verge of dying, was often lying on a litter on the dirt floor of my mother's house, a house that, like all the old Berber houses of Azro Wado (valley of the Ammelns), was made of pink granite, the color of the surrounding mountains. These old houses stood up against the most punishing weather; they were generally two stories, with the ground floor made up of an angular courtyard, a barn, a roundish oven made of clay, a henhouse (*tagourt*), several stalls and low rooms for storing hay and firewood . . .

Back then, the Berber home was the center of a circle (*douar* or village) that was generally quite large. It was the ultimate building block. It was called the hearth (*Kanoun*)—though this term also had a sociological significance. The village was only as valuable as the cohesion of the cells or hearths that composed it, just like a healthy body. Its fundamental structure was like a well-tuned musical instrument. No false note could be tolerated—only a true harmony could allow for community solidarity. Even though the tribe was led by a civil assessor at the time, the villages managed to maintain their individuality. There was a *Jemâa* (a council) that presided over ordinary business. This small assembly governed absolutely everything, though I wouldn't say they brought the rain or good weather. However, they were the tuning fork of the village.

The role of the Elders, and this included women, was major. A grandmother carried as much weight as any patriarch. They were, between them, the true cement that bonded the community to its mythic past. A grandmother didn't veil herself outside the home. Always clad in an ample black sheet, hair held up by a red scarf (*akenbouch*) bound by a black headband embroidered with coral branches, she saw to all sorts of domestic operations and chatted, equal to equal, with the men who respected her advanced age and her cultural memory transmitted through time's long night.

My grandmother spoke from the heart of the night, on the terrace of our house, while I studied the summer sky shuddering with millions of stars. And I followed the paths of meteors without losing an iota of this music issuing from the depths of the ages. She fascinated and terrified me all at once. It was at this point in the year when my grandmother would spin the immaculate wool she'd washed with soapwort and meticulously carded. Then, she'd pull out of some dark room an impressive loom and then she'd be at it, making as if by magic our winter clothes. From her thin fingers emerged cloaks (*selhams*), gandouras and other burnouses that kept us, my grandfather and I, warm even in the most intense cold. This admirable grandparent took care of basically everything. She weeded the vegetable gardens in the valley two or three kilometers from home. She presided over various sowings, because she alone knew how to choose the best seedlings. She never let anyone else make the daily barley couscous besides her. In spring, she brightened workaday Berber meals with the delicious and tender stalks and leaves of young turnip greens (*couscous waw'sai*).

To see this image today is to be washed again in the pure light of childhood and to inhale its old smoke. My grandmother didn't gather wood on the mountain. She didn't milk or feed the cow, nor did she take care of the donkey, even though she loved animals and fed, straight out of her hands, the chicks from each new brood: little pincushions as yellow as the yellowest canary. The role of my grandmother wasn't to govern but to simply be present. Just her existence was comforting. She was a vibrant shimmer of the past, the present, and the future. But her nearly ethereal physiognomy, her spindly, vanishing, intangible but smiling body, worried me at the same time it reassured me, because it was full of eternity. So it was that I was afraid of losing my grandmother, but gradually, as I grew up, I grew away from her. A long time after her accidental death, she continued to appear in my dreams along the undulating countryside of childhood where she'd spoken to me in several languages while initiating me in the ways of the flora and fauna.

My grandmother and my mother coexisted peacefully. No doubt this was due to their considerable difference in age. You got married very young in those days. But there was also the legendary wisdom of my grandparent. My mother, her beauty Atlassian and somewhat Saharan, like all the Berber women of the time, took care of all sorts of drudgery both inside and out: wood and water duty, sowing and reaping, shaking the almond trees, huge weekly washing, and so on. Basically, she worked hard and never objected. I didn't come to understand this until the day she weaned me, after the birth of my younger brother. She offered me a breast coated in juniper oil to help rid me of the taste for her milk. I gave it one suck and started bawling like a madman. A couple of days later, I accepted the new situation. I got used to solid foods. One spring, my mother brought me a rabbit kit she'd caught in the fields. I played with it like a toy, but I was so clumsy I ended up breaking its neck. Seeing it stop hopping and instead flopping around in a pitiful attempt at moving, I burst out sobbing. Another time, my mother gave me a full-grown hare who'd lost its head. "I tore it from a jackal," she told me. And then she cooked it on a brazier.

What I wouldn't give for another moment like that! If there was ever anyone who was linked viscerally to the earth of their birth, it was my mother. She knew every crease and secret the mountain had; she knew everything about the occult activities of *jnouns,* the diurnal and nocturnal spirits, and she identified them easily at the bend of a path or in impossible places like the debris of shattered rocks or the residues of streams thick with insects and leeches. I have her to thank for a large portion of my imagination. She inducted me into the arcana of the land, and even though she was illiterate, she knew how to decipher the signs in Nature's huge book. I don't doubt that she gave me, maybe without knowing it, a certain understanding not of texts but of the fruit of experience and memory. Without the daily labor of these kinds of unknown women, what would have become of the Berber children, what would have become of these mountainfolk who needed to tear their subsistence out

of arid soil and rock? Up until recently they were the real eco-
nomic agents of these remote villages. Tough peasants, bent by
the most off-putting tasks, they overcame and ended up con-
quering the precarity of their existence all while safeguarding an
essentially oral cultural history that's on its way, now, toward
vanishing. Same as this land, by the way, no longer cultivated
and from which one no longer expects much of anything at all.

TRASH

For Mohammed Allal Sinaceur,
my old friend

At the edge of the large historic town humming with glittery lives, and all along the raised trainway, hills of household garbage grow around hundred-year-old palm trees that only yield, these days, a dry and bitter fruit.

Myriad storks populate this filthy vastness offered up to the turquoise sky and the weary eye of the impenitent traveler who's already wiped other storms with other shameful images. He had long ago crossed this trash heap of a tumultuous megalopolis, several strata high and hiding from view as far as the eye can see a landscape once strewn with copses and rustling with the sweet rhythm of flowing streams.

Today, only a lost cow would graze this rank plateau.

On either side of the road that leads to a countryside a little bit less ravaged by the stains of civilization, dumpsters pour out all the great city has thrown out once it's extracted the vital substance from it.

And from time to time bulldozers come and flatten it all out, in order to compress this enormous human secretion. A blackish liquid seeps out of it in rivulets and sticky tracks that the sun, mute witness to daily catastrophes, tints with the consummate skill of a master who could make from a repulsive carcass an object worthy of lofty, indispensable desires.

When the wind rises, these empires of muck inflate their thin plastic bags that fly along in wobbly spirals, many of them snagging in the branches of stunted shrubs like so many offerings to a frantic, sickly modernity.

Elsewhere, along the periphery of the great European cities, the sumptuous garbage of the societies of waste and surfeit house colonies of gulls who have found a bounty of available food much richer than the meager produce of maritime leftovers. These birds, remarkable trash collectors, have crossed hundreds of kilometers, attracted who knows how by the pestilential odor of this endless feast.

Municipal or illegal dumps, these dubious jewels of the civilization of the stomach circumscribe a nature that has nothing left of itself but its name.

In other places, manufacturers, frothing for profit, sometimes dig pits where they dump toxic waste that directly threatens the groundwater. These godlings without belief or humility are like enormous drug addicts who'd rather live a single moment of pure euphoria than enjoy the little pricks of a parsimonious pleasure as rare as the hypothetical product of a dedicated gold-panner.

Voices, always the same ones, rise over the heaps to announce the next end of civilization and the likely inauguration of a barbarity more fearsome than the nearby tribal wars that the former warring nations watch like a ballet of dangerous, untouchable vipers.

No one's going to intervene in these bloody quarrels unless it's to exhume mass graves, heaps of bodies disfigured, purple and putrid who not long ago were peaceful men out of whose guts a hateful demon surged, transforming them into implacable enemies, then proud and ruthless combatants, and then, finally, into cadavers buried in the open air.

All these trash heaps are the work of this biped that will never be done with justifying its crimes in the name of a cause lost long in advance.

Here is where egotism, craving, and violence rule.

SOME KIND OF PARIS

In Paris, in the year 19**, two homeless men in the prime of their lives were lying beneath the meager verdure of one of the three trees planted right in the middle of the Place de la Contrescarpe. Several wine bottles had rolled into the gutter, one of which was still half full. A large puddle of vomit (not the homeless men's) marked with a blue and yellow tinge the edge of the sidewalk just in front of The Tankard, the café where Zanuck had once come to film some scenes for a movie. Back then, Zanuck had been giddy, sly, immersed in the actors' work and the director's gesticulations and suggestions; seated in the driver's seat of a Rolls Royce, he was sucking on a fat Havana while squinting into the brasserie where they were filming, in front of the rapt crowd gathered around the plaza, a scene where a large woman was chugging a liter of red wine before the twinkling eyes of three goons with huge tattooed biceps.

One of the sots was sleeping off, with snoring vigor, a ferocious bender. The kind of binge that lifts up the misfits and armchair philosophers who only see society as a troubled sea rife with shoals ready to scuttle the lives of small, certainly brave, but incredibly fragile, serfs.

Those days, the ghoul of unemployment, whose monstrous silhouette loomed above the horizon of trade wars and armed conflicts, was only clocked by those rare minds supposed to glimpse and interpret the future's secrets.

These people were neither prophets nor miracle workers— just men and women sensitive to the world's developing story. They perceived inside the smallest detail the hidden actions of the social body; they derived conscious enjoyment from political failures and the collapse of demagogues, though they never took lightly the social tensions and oriental wars on which the well-being of the Occident was predicated. But we're not even there yet; unemployment was scaring no one. We were still in an era of prosperous calm, between a rock and a hard place, because the raw materials and boundless energy from the Third World still cost next to nothing. Paris has always been a movable feast (Hemingway)—the air was soft, almost voluptuous; the winters harsh but poetic.

We warmed ourselves with charcoal and woodfire, as in the olden days; the poorest had oil-burning stoves and the richest had heating systems worthy of the finest international palaces. There were still knife-grinders with pan flutes whistling out strange notes and itinerant glaziers whose calls reverberated against the facades of buildings that were being restored little by little; and then, not far from Contrescarpe, there was the Jardin des Plantes, with its many well-cared-for animals, its centuries-old trees, among them a cedar of Lebanon well over two hundred years old, and other Judean trees whose biblical names hypnotized the poets, those ardent readers of buried symbols. And the birds! Raptors, ostriches, parrots, technicolor macaws. And all of those lemurs, like the Malagasy maki you loved to pet and that accepted the treats you never forgot to bring him. And the crow that recognized your footsteps from way off, the one that called you Florent because he'd confused you with a zoo worker. And the lonely lion locked up in its enclosure that never stopped watching the entrance because he was always waiting in vain but with a fervent hope for a visit from his former owner, a doctor whose arm he had literally ripped off because the owner had foolishly entered the cage without ensuring that the beast knew it was him, and so the lion mistook the doctor for an intruder or enemy, which is why he leapt on him with such frenzy. He would have finished him off if he hadn't abruptly realized that this man who was very quickly losing consciousness was his benefactor, friend, and owner. This magnificent creature looked at no one, his eyes trained on the main entrance of the enclosure, but the man whom the lion loved with an inexpressible love had, they said, refused to ever set eyes again on the animal he'd given to the Jardin des Plantes after his horrific accident.

You lived those days at the end of the rue Mouffetard, at number 3 on Post Office Way; you didn't sleep much those days because you loved to wander during the golden hour along the

Contrescarpe and then far beyond there; you ambled along the Seine's quays, muttering to yourself the poems Baudelaire had dedicated to the tranquil river and Parisian mornings he'd loved so much. You stopped often to chew the fat with the anglers, some of whom would periodically joggle their poles baited with old Gruyère, pulling barbels of decent size now and then from the murky water.

You were surprised anyone could find fish here of such notable length, knowing as you did that the Seine for so long had been not much more than a sewer and even a colossal trash can in which you could find, in the mounding silt, old cars, mopeds, mattresses, strollers, skeletons, firearms used in holdups or unsolved murders—in a word, everything an ailing society might consider a worthless or compromising object and thus worthy of hurling. But you, you loved this side of Paris, the Paris that today has been handed over to the anarchy of speculation and the misery the sad, delinquent suburbs dump onto the City of Lights that no blemish can ever taint, because it's known terrible disasters and has always surged out of them like the Phoenix flaring eternally out of its own ashes, reborn.

Paris! You are the homeless poet's true homeland, and also, of course, his grave.

REPTILES

For Mehdi El Mandjra,
my insightful friend

It had been a long night, one that lasted millions of years, during which the reptile in all its forms was the undisputed master of the Planet. Once it left the primordial Ocean behind, it evolved on land and in the air with such remarkable ease that it grew to a monumental size, clumsy but troubling. It wasn't much more, really, than a ravenous machine unable to react quickly or smoothly, because it didn't have a brain big enough to match its impressive size; instead, by the time information made its way to its tiny reptilian brain, its tail or some other part of its enormous body was in the carnivorous jaws of a tyrannosaurus or another behemoth sowing panic among the phlegmatic herds of herbivorous dinosaurs. However, not every one of these antediluvian lizards was huge; there were little ones, too, like the pisanosaurus, whose small size helped it survive. And then there were some that were even more miniscule who weren't more than a couple dozen centimeters in size. But the human imagination can only really remember from this period the enormity of these creatures who overran the planetary night and who crash through our dreams and terrify us, as if the ontological angst we are so familiar with dates back to these unbiblical ages where life and death duked it out without end. And then came the inevitable: a disaster—a cataclysm caused by a huge asteroid or a sudden and brutal glaciation striking the globe—sweeping away in no time at all everything but the memory of these fantastic beings whose towering silhouettes dominated the bucolic landscapes and limpid lakes sparkling in the humid sunshine of this tropical era tempered, slightly, by a perpetual vernal breeze. Only the little beasts, those who had never meant that much, were able to adapt to the new conditions that ruled the environment as it weathered the climatic shifts and the complex chemistry of the fundamental life processes laying the groundwork for an uncertain future.

A constant, ruthless struggle, visible and invisible, wore on for the domination or just the base survival of the remaining species; only the insect made it out of this eternal war unscathed, having always exercised an unchallenged reign nothing else could ever touch, naturally armed as it was against the bad luck that had trapped other species who were as leathery as they were fragile, thanks to the complicated parameters of a Nature whose instability was part of its resistance to all exogenous entropies. In the Big Book of the Universe, syntax and semantics are an atomic order; they subdivide infinitely in such a way that even the reader of stars or quasars can fathom this magnificent text which is the basis of the most immeasurable things. And how could this reader, as aware and nearly as mystical as the Sufi, not be struck dumb by the might and amplitude of this uninterrupted design? "God," he says to himself, "has made a place in his heart for all his creatures, including the lowest. He loves all he has made, but we erstwhile philosophers and anchorites are so far from anything which is not ourselves, which is a mortal sin." The holy man who thought this way wasn't a confirmed enemy of life; rather, he knew how to measure the degree of the imperfections that have condemned him to a long and severe asceticism.

An asceticism that he was ready to continue throughout the Beyond for the Glorification of the Creator of worlds. Friend to mild creatures and huge beasts of land and air, the Saint had a particular preference for the reptiles that moved along on their stomachs by contracting their annular muscles in the manner of ophidians or by clawing their way up the hillock or rugged rock in the manner of the particolored lizard who celebrates summer with the splendor of its scaly robe. This Saint who walked day and night in the footsteps of an unknown ancestor enjoyed charming serpents and rattlesnakes, centipedes and other myriapods who, it's been said, would only release those whom they've bitten once they've been presented with a basketful of gold pieces. This story, familiar to all denizens of the South, reveals an old superstition born from a ritual that was once commonplace among the tribes of huntresses that the Roman empire never managed to conquer.

And because myths and legends have a thick skin, the Sufi Saint, clad in rough wool, was constantly correcting the warped vision of the uneducated whose mountainous isolation reinforced their ignorance and gullibility; they believed, as a matter of fact, in the existence of male and female demons who oversaw works and days like impartial and invisible company heads. For his part, the Saint believed in djinns with two sexes, as the Koran invoked them liberally. "There are djinns who believe and there are djinns who do not," he'd state. "Only the demons who abet evil are damned forever by the Creator and his prophets. For me, the demon can be both visible and invisible at once; as for the *djin*, it remains an impalpable and ectoplasmic creature, without any material existence, which does not, however, prevent it from appearing as a crisp image in the human imagination. An image which, in comparison to the terrifying image of the demon, is rather soothing."

A circle of old women listened attentively to the Saint. The village was drowsing through the summery heat of the afternoon, but the elders were not napping. This was the time of the year when a saint would visit this place hemmed in by two craggy ridges of unusual height. The only way to access the village was via a particularly treacherous mule track. Further down, in the valley, verdant fields spread out along a sparkling stream. Those who had made their fortunes in trade, in some distant city unknown to the villagers who'd stayed behind, had come back and built villas in the valley, as no one had any reason to fear the sudden attacks of bandits anymore, as they'd disappeared long ago. They had infested the region during the Seïba, that turbulent period where everyone was armed and could kill without risking prison or death. You could be killed as easily for owning a fruit tree as you could over a border dispute. The strongest, which is to say the most well-armed, always got the better of the most defenseless. One of these former strongmen, who had killed without any regard, still lived in a kind of small fort that was basically an impregnable citadel. All you could see from the outside was a high wall with regular arrow slits, a wall of stones so immense it easily resisted the most intense assaults.

The old killer never went to the mosque, despite having made the pilgrimage to Mecca; he didn't mix anymore with the people and was never seen at holy festivals. But he was still feared. Even though he'd gotten on in years, he was only spoken of in low tones and innuendo, because it was said he still controlled occult forces more dangerous than lightning. From time to time, this old man who was rarely seen would walk out onto the terrace of his abode to hold, in his swiveling gaze, the two mountains that cradled the valley, clasping it upstream and downstream like an abrupt and jumbled granite vise. He only had a dim idea of what the valley had become, but his sharp memory still enclosed within it scenes that had made his reputation as an invincible cutthroat. "I have skin as thick as the hide of an antediluvian saurian. No wound, not even a mortal one, has gotten the better of my carcass," he loved to repeat to himself, and he'd often add, upon seeing one of his brothers, flesh rotted by gangrene and teeming with worms, "What a pity!"

Then, he'd grit his teeth and curse that goddamned porcupine that had injured his firstborn and stuck a long quill in his thigh. "A warrior must only die at the hands of a warrior who's stronger or craftier, not thanks to the poisoned quill of a lowly porcupine!" His thoughts, or rather his imagination, traveled far back in space and time, and he saw among scenes of incredible savagery the titanic scuffle of hazy combatants—hulking monsters raised up on the massive, towering pillars of their hind legs. "I must have been one of these giants," it pleased the old killer to say in his heart of hearts. "No doubt at all." He was illiterate and knew nothing of the mythical existence of juggernauts and fantastic beasts, but his unconscious reproduced what his limited intelligence refused to let in, namely, a bestiary that no sensible human can behold without feeling seized by an unspeakable fear that comes directly from their lemurian ancestors, tiny mammals no bigger than a middling beetle or a dwarf hummingbird. "Yes," the killer told himself, "I only slaughtered in self-defense. And I will swear this to God on the day of the last judgment."

But the holy Sufi, who knew all of human history since the flood, knew that this godless old man was going to join in Gehenna those wicked beings who had flooded the entire earth with agony and blood. "He will join his peers in the eternal furnace," the holy man said. And he picked up his staff to set off on his interminable journey, far from men and the harshness of Destiny.

"I am as the serpent, I change my skin regularly, though it is my soul that improves," he mused as, exhausted and famished, he stretched out on his back at the bottom of a hole and placed a large stone on his stomach to quiet the spasms of his empty gullet.

CATASTROPHES AND PLAGUES

For my old friend Ahmed M'jad

"The village has endured," the priest sings in a funereal voice that turns the heart of each elder in the audience to stone. The church is an old ship no tempest has succeeded in ripping the mast from, a Santa Maria stuck on its rock by the powerful hands of a god from before the first Flood: the stained-glass windows are as gaunt as the wretches they depict, poor wrecked villagers lifting beseeching eyes to the sky. Besides the muffled voice of the vicar, no sound disturbs the privacy of the place. Outside, a disturbing murmur like the roar of some apocalyptic monster. The celebrants know it's the river swollen with stormwater that's howling as if possessed by an inextinguishable fury. During summer it wasn't more than a thin shoelace of stagnant water teeming with larvae and anopheles; there was little hope then it would swell again with the rain that is the farmer's nectar and ambrosia. Come autumn, the first storm darkened the sky's high vault, throwing over the village a cope so heavy even the animals preferred the dark barn to the fields; the people barricaded themselves in and trembled, praying the sky wouldn't fall in on them; but the sky didn't listen to them, thunder rumbled through days and nights, and torrents of water rushed down the slopes; the river swelled and then flooded with such intensity that it carried off like wisps of straw the cottages the city slickers had built along its banks. There were deaths and disappearances; tapers were lit and sobbed over but nothing could dam the scourge only the elders knew to fear and respect.

In other latitudes, calamities bear strange names like Daisy, Mary, Fanny. The names of femmes fatales, or the names of epic poets, like Hugo . . . Thus the cyclones and typhoons are baptized, as if this might strip from them the violence that demolishes the buildings of men and God carried off by blasts of wind.

Under yet other skies, catastrophes are called famine, acridian invasions, civil wars, and the loss of the notion of space and time; there, men disembowel one another for a fistful of rice or a swallow of muddy water, because these countries both distant and near don't experience floods and know storms only as barren rumblings.

These rough beings count their dead and shed no tears. They only say that the dead are happier than the living. They don't accuse the rich whom they've never seen; they pray and perish inside an indifference broken occasionally by the cameramen or doctors airdropped from another galaxy, foreign eyes that feast on the world's woes.

TWO CUTTHROATS

Back then, the mountains were in a lather. Tribes were warring over peanuts, and clans were organizing punitive raids against other clans they'd feuded with for generations. From this shapeless magma, which you might say resembled the disorganization of two anthills fighting to control a tight scrap of land, a man of average size emerged, stout and solid as the trunk of an argan tree. He feared no man or thing, because his impetuous weapons were the best expression of the only law recognized throughout the land, namely, that death came for those stubborn enough to contest the boss's will.

This thug lived cut off from the rest of the world in a kind of impregnable fortress whose high wall overlooked the main watercourse irrigating the valley. Out of respect, he was known as The Killer, an honorable title in this era of upheaval when everyone worked hard to get along with their peers, even if it meant abandoning an asset for the benefit of the mightier. It was better to hold onto your life than to any wealth coveted by the godless, lawless, sometimes parentless (and roofless) brutes. Some twisted minds insinuated that The Killer was none other than the head of a band of fearsome thieves who robbed travelers before cutting them to ribbons. It was said these guys were like those vicious dogs who attack solitary timid passersby, the sickly kind of creature that secretes an odor so particular and so irksome you may as well ring the dinner bell for every nearby beast. However, this dangerous man wasn't in charge of any band, because there weren't any in the area; at most, he connived with a sidekick known familiarly as The Butcher who had once eviscerated a baby while its mother was holding it in her arms, just so that the bloodline of his enemy would be scrubbed from the face of the earth forever. The Butcher was crueler than The Killer, whom he considered a kindred spirit, because the latter only executed people for precise reasons while the other thought of them merely as cows on their hind legs. Obviously he had a rifle, but he preferred to use his *koummya,* with its engraved silver knob. The bluish shimmers of the weapon's sparkling blade evoked a twinge of pity in him whenever some braggart got in its way.

"What's with this frenzy when you kill?" The Killer asked.

"It's stronger than me," The Butcher replied. "Could be something to do with my old job."

"Everyone knows you were the best butcher for a dozen miles in every direction, but to go from that to killing poor bastards for free . . ."

"What do you mean? You think I'm off my rocker."

"Not in the slightest, my friend. I just think that you're not exercising enough self-control. Could be you just happen to love the scent and sight of blood. People like you, we call them vampires. But you don't drink the blood, you're just happy to spill it."

"Ah, blood. It's true, I'm obsessed with it. May it please heaven that the river that runs the length of the wall of your compound transforms into a long and torrential current of blood. Then I could bathe in it and wash myself clean of all the world's trash. I love to see the blood of beasts run, and even more the blood of cowards. It's a gas."

"All that'll get you is the contempt and primal hatred of others. Not to mention all the orphans and widows you've made lately."

"Ah, you don't get it. There's a joy I get from it you others don't understand. An Edenic joy no one else could understand. No other pleasure could even hold a candle to it."

Sometimes they'd set off on expeditions, perched on their mule, cresting the steepest passes on their way to villages rumored to harbor hidden treasure, though more often than not it was only a handful of women and assorted scrawny geezers. Once, though, they discovered a bag of doubloons in the home of an old Jew whose life they spared but whose only daughter they raped before the horrified eyes of her parents. It was only later they learned their victim was a ruthless loan shark who'd forced many a family into ruin. The rape wasn't a crime to them;

it meant nothing to them so long as it didn't touch them. Especially since the Jewish virgin, along with her parents, could consider themselves all settled up, having gotten out of it alive and without any more damage than the theft and rape, which were as common as air during that time of total uncertainty. The Butcher had wanted to cut their throats, of course, as was his wont, but The Killer vigorously dissuaded him.

"We've got nothing against these people, they're not our enemies," he explained. "If you touch so much as a hair on their heads, it'll cost you. Not only did they offer us kindness, but we also got this tidy little fortune. There's enough here to get no small amount of new gear. The smugglers from the north are selling beautiful English rifles, repeating ones that can hold a good number of rounds. You don't have to reload after each shot. They kill quick and clean. What about a visit to Agadir? Maybe the souks around it too? No doubt we'll find something to satisfy us."

He'd already decided. He would make his way to the port town of Agadir.

"Oh, no. I'd never go to that city," The Butcher responded. "It's crawling with *roumis* and cops. I don't feel like getting stopped like some small-time crook."

"You're that scared of a thing like prison? You've got it wrong, my man. No one there knows who you are. You forget that our mountain is an eagle's nest and is under nobody's control but our own. Don't be so anxious. You can walk around that town without any worries."

"Ha! I reek of blood. I'm a bloodletter. No official with half a brain could fail to sniff me out. Trouble finds me, I'm telling you. It's better I don't go, trust me."

"Your loss, then. Here's your share of the loot," The Killer said as he handed The Butcher a small clutch of gold pieces.

Never in his life had he seen so much money sparkle in one place. It might have been this unexpected wealth that made him say:

"Let's say I did go. There must be good-looking women and good drinking wine there. I've had enough of the Jews' *mahia*, not to mention the whores, too. Fetid as a wild boar's den."

"There he is!" The Killer exclaimed. "Off we go, then. We've got nothing else to do here or in the village. We'll get supplies along the way."

They took an old caravan route rarely used in those days and gathered provisions at the home of a man who, thanks to their gruesome appearance, was quick to welcome them like pilgrims. After that, they tried to look the part of travelers headed east. They even declared they were on their way to board an ocean liner in Tangiers, which added to their status.

In doing this, they displayed their weapons, not in order to scare people but to demonstrate that they knew how to defend themselves should any aggressors pop out. Nevertheless, no one dared ask them about where they came from, let alone their social status.

All anyone knew was that they were dealing with a couple of unusual guys. The Killer in particular inspired a vague, almost visceral terror, thanks to his blazing eyes and his salt-and-pepper mustache curled at the ends like a fat scorpion's tail. When they were hungry and far from any town, they hunted rabbits, which they flushed with stones from stands of date trees where all kinds of rodents nested. The Killer, a crack shot, always hit his prey before it had leapt the ten times necessary to get out of reach. But one time they had to settle for the fat lizards the locals called whip-tails in these hinterlands. They roasted and ate them, because the area they were trekking through was so stony and arid it housed nothing but scorpions, snakes, and other reptiles, one more venomous than the next. They never lacked for water, though, as each had a goatskin full of water bouncing against the flank of their mount. Sometimes they spent the night in caves, other times under a tree; while one slept, the other stood watch.

One time, however, a tramp took the risk of hanging around them; without a clue as to who they were, he threatened to sic all the demons in hell on them if they didn't feed him. It was a bad move, as The Butcher thrashed him senseless and left him for dead on the ground. As they were packing up camp, The Killer said to his accomplice:

"You ought to wake that bastard up."

"Why? If the jackals and hyenas want any, he'll get gobbled up. But he reeks too much even for those creatures, the vilest among the whole of creation."

And so they left without looking back. The tramp was unconscious, though he wasn't in much danger, seeing as dawn had just broken and the real beasts didn't hunt until night. It's said of the hyena that it will only attack a wounded or weakened man it knows will lose his sangfroid as it walks in shrinking circles around him as it cackles savagely. They even say the hyena will then urinate on its prey, which then must follow the hyena docilely back to its lair in order to be ripped to shreds.

A *moghazni* on night duty by a public building in Bouizakarne, right on the edge of the Sahara, reported that as soon as a hyena is in the vicinity, every dog runs for cover and hides, trembling something fierce because the scavenger could eat each of them for breakfast if it got hold of them. This primal fear shatters the will of even the most ferocious guard dog. Among the people of the South, the hyena is the symbol of all things cruel and sly. Whoever travels at night better have their eyes open and one hand on a good weapon. Anyone bivouacking better light a fire, too, in order to ward off these creatures attracted to equine scent, and you better keep an ear out, too, for the slightest crack of a twig. One time, and one time only, The Killer had to deal with a couple of starving hyenas who had been following his mule. In order to preclude their attack, he'd tied his mount to a juniper tree and had lain on a rock to take aim at and dispatch them—a simple matter for a marksman of his stripe. Then he blew them away, extracted their brains from their skulls, and dressed them. He sold everything to a druggist known for his remedies and magic potions, because the brain and hide of a hyena are an important part of the traditional pharmacopoeia and its various enchantments. Plenty of men and women have gone mad after unwittingly consuming the brain of this animal both feared and reviled. It's said that someone who is speaking loudly must have eaten this scavenger's brain. The gelatinous material is known for its psychotropic properties as well as its toxins, which are as deadly as arsenic or the poisonous secretions of the datura, those madness- and death-inducing substances that go so well with mint and tea and the destruction of one's enemies. Whoever knows this can no longer trust anyone, nor can they eat or drink anything they don't prepare themselves. This sinister period was one of bloody account settling, of stubborn feuds dividing clans and even families who had seemed before so tightly knit. Brothers were killing each other for less than nothing, though no one was surprised, since cruelty was the norm for this time of famine and general instability. Everywhere was in the grip of a drought so deep that the poor were obliged to eat dry carrots and weevil-eaten barley that the women threshed at high noon under a merciless sun, the better to separate each grain from the tough bugs the rats competed with in the lofts; some dug up bland tubers and roots in order to quiet their hunger, while many others, who were completely ignorant of the characteristics of the plants they'd ingested, fell ill and, in order to recover, had to resort to the herbal remedies of the *fquihs,* who had long ago mastered the medicinal secrets of plants. The scarcity of food was so severe that any man old enough to bear arms migrated north, where, it was said, there was food in abundance. They worked like mules, laboring under the command of foremen who made them sweat, but they were hardy and frugal and many a laborer was able to open a stall in the medina. Others wasted their pay in brothels and bars, concluding their frantic run in sanatoria, dying far from the warmth of family, in total anonymity. Their original community had lost them long ago. Those who escaped tuberculosis and other terrible illnesses slaved away like convicts and never made it back home, where it was said they were probably dead and buried. No one even bothered to ask around about them. In the village, their locked houses fell deeper into ruin as the years wore on, when they weren't occupied by foreigners chased out of the Sahel by famine and drought. Among those, some had become such an integral part of the valley that many thought of them as family. They were the ones entrusted with the heaviest fieldwork, the drilling of wells, and the building of houses. Surprising that a nomad could build a house, someone who had only known a hide tent for a home, but these foreigners had learned architecture and masonry from the Dogons, and whoever knew them well enough knew that they had descended from the ancient lords of the Empire of Mali. This legendary trait is what distinguished them from the Haratin and other Africans of diverse ethnic backgrounds. However, all these wanderers were welcomed in the village like distant brothers, for they espoused unconditionally the causes of their adoptive tribe. They were often good masons, reputable well-diggers, able blacksmiths, experienced cobblers, skilled farmers, and intrepid warriors. They knew how to use firearms, blades, and even bows. They were excellent horsemen, and woe to those who crossed swords with them during close combat. They could be trusted, because they were as avid as fresh recruits to prove themselves in battle, much more than any hardened vet; they earned respect and sometimes a small fortune along with it, enough to purchase a small herd of goats or sheep. They were superb herdsmen. They loved and respected their animals. They produced sheep's milk and sometimes goat's, too, though they didn't make cheese because they weren't even aware it existed. Their only true enemy was the lingering drought that forced them to the souk to sell off their flock, which they immediately saw led off to the slaughterhouse. They never ate the flesh of the animals they raised, which had almost become members of their family, though whenever a distinguished guest came by, they didn't hesitate to sacrifice a ram with which to make a *mechoui* bright with green peppercorns, fresh thyme, and ground cumin. Whenever that happened, it was a feast, with women singing and dancing all night around a bonfire to the sound of tambourines they beat with expert, rhythmic hands. A celebration through the night, under a sun shattered into stars dripping with the plasmic light of the cosmos, like an oasis of life in the middle of a shadowy desert riddled with traps. Those nights, you could feel the complete fragility of the human condition, as well as a strange sympathy for one's fellow man tangled up with dread and repressed tenderness, because it is hard to think of oneself as anything significant in the face of the fathomless infinity in which each being, each elementary particle, nevertheless had its own place of honor.

Neither The Killer nor The Butcher ever took part in these celebrations, though they were hardly forgotten. Every time there was any kind of banquet, a suckling lamb was sacrificed

for them and brought along on a platter made of walnut. This
was done in order to secure their protection, because they were
the only leaders of the region. Whenever one of these roasts
was held, The Butcher summoned a Jew to act as his sommelier.

"Pour me a little of that good *mahia*, Mardukh, or I'll roll
you off to hell," he said, adding immediately after, "And get
yourself some of that leg of lamb, you old crook."

Mardukh was a saddlemaker by trade, but he also knew how
to make the finest brandy, having, as he did (in addition to a
couple of tricks behind his kindling, as the distillers have it in
their parlance), an alembic in perfect working order.

"You are some kind of glutton and drunk," The Killer said,
teasing his companion. "I don't drink, I don't smoke, and I eat
in moderation. I think you know who between us will see a
hundred."

Then they burst out laughing, because they both knew that
one day some killer more cunning than both of them would
send them to the Devil.

"We're going to get old as hobbling boars in our corners of
the sty," they told themselves in order to downplay the dangers
all around them.

But that night, they didn't sleep. Both were watching their
surroundings, which they'd mined with traps, having spent the
whole day hungry and luckless in the hunt thanks to the crushing heat. They made do with a little cornmeal biscuit that wasn't
enough for a child. Where they'd hunkered down at the moment seemed like it should be crawling with game. It had to be
true, because scattered everywhere was fresh jackrabbit scat. So
they'd decided to give it a shot and place their snares not far from
camp. And so they strove to dissolve into the growing, silent
shadows. The intermittent cracking of sunbaked stones cooling
off periodically broke the night's enormous silence as they tuned
their ears to the slightest stirring of dried grass or spiny bush.
Suddenly, they heard clear as day the characteristic sound of a
human cough. It couldn't be anything else. "That's a man," they
said at the same time. They continued waiting, their rifles closer
to hand as a precaution. But the cough disappeared. Since they
felt the need, now, to split, they readied themselves for the next

leg of the trek, after which The Killer went off to inspect the area. Not too far off, he saw a small glimmer flashing between two rocks, then two shadows he couldn't quite make out. He set off straightaway to make sure that whatever they were, they weren't a threat. And so he sank into obscurity with exceeding care, because he didn't want to stumble over some stone or stump and unquestionably wake the attention of the two he aimed to surprise. As he drew closer, he could hear snatches of words, and though he couldn't tell what was being said, he knew he was dealing with a couple of highwaymen. He didn't lump himself in with these scoundrels. He had a sense of honor, and if he fleeced the rich or took out his enemies, it was in order to impose his will and power on those other tribes who would have attacked his own if his strength was not well demonstrated. And so he held these lowlifes in contempt for their cowardly attacks on travelers, lone women, and defenseless geezers. "Well," he said to himself, "I better give these two a thorough going over." And so he pushed on with new purpose. Rifle cocked, he walked right up to the two, who hadn't noticed anything out of the ordinary.

"Hey!" he yelled. "You're surrounded, you yellow-bellied cowards! You're going to get what's been coming to you. You'll regret having ever been born."

"But we haven't done you any wrong," one of them protested. "What do you want from us? We're just a couple of simple travelers, that's all."

"All I see is a couple of low-class gutter-loving thieves. I bet you just finished stuffing your saddlebags with some poor widow's loot. And if the size of those bags is to be believed" (he pointed at two bags on the ground), "then you must have made out pretty darn well. But that's not what we're talking about here. Your time is up, gents."

At that, the hoodlum who'd acted befuddled reached for a revolver holstered on his left leg, but The Killer fired first, shattering his right hand.

"That'll teach you to clown around," he said as his victim howled, rolling around on the stony ground.

"Open the bags!" he ordered the other thief.

"But those are ours . . ."

"So? You want a taste of what your friend just got? Go on, hop to it!"

He opened the bags without another word. It was clear The Killer wasn't joking.

"Well, well, isn't this a sight for sore eyes. Caftans stitched and spangled with gold and silver. These must cost a pretty penny. Where'd you score these? Tell me quick or you'll be eating lead!"

"Oh, well, um, we robbed an old Jewish merchant up the road from here."

"You're lying!"

"I swear upon the Koran! You can see for yourself—there's a picture of him in those bags."

"Ok, ok, I believe you. Not that it makes a difference, since you're already dead."

"But . . ."

He didn't have a chance to finish his sentence. Behind him, the enormous shadow of The Butcher suddenly appeared and, seizing his head, slit his throat in a single motion with an expert hand. The other thief suffered the same fate.

"Crime doesn't pay," The Killer stated.

It was abundantly clear that the loot of these two thieves they'd summarily executed would fetch The Killer and his accomplice a lot of money. They had a rough sense of what they'd get for it. They would sell the two dead men's animals along with everything they'd worn or carried—their clothes, jewels, and weapons. It would fetch a tidy sum, allowing The Butcher to have a blast at the brothels and The Killer to round out his collection of rifles with a couple new additions of recent make. But they were still far from the city where these enterprises presided.

The peak before them seemed at times insurmountable, though they knew all of its paths and felt confident in their veteran's instinct that nothing else lay in store for them. It was now merely a question of days.

The journey felt long because they only traveled a couple of hours in the morning in order to avoid the worst effects of the stifling heat. They didn't want their animals to suffer from thirst, nor did they want to risk heatstroke for themselves. High

summer, and the heat made waves in the air that danced a ballet
fit for a devil's mass.

During the most sweltering hours, they tied the mules up in
the shadow of a huge argan tree and stretched themselves out
in a nearby crevice, reveling in the cool air's relief. Beyond, only
the chirps of grasshoppers and the screech of crickets reigned
in a world otherwise apparently devoid of life. This was the
time of day when they could risk a nap without fear of prowl-
ers, because no one was crazy enough to roam around beneath
a leaden sun. After eating some of their leftovers from the last
hunt, they gulped down a couple mouthfuls of water and shared
a cup of tea (no mint) before bedding down on a smooth, flat
stone to cool their overheated bodies and grab a couple of rest-
ful winks. That night, they resumed their silent trek beneath a
moon that lit each rock's smallest nub. They enjoyed drinking
in the evening air, full of mingled scents. They walked behind
their mules for hours without tiring. They were full of vigor and
ready to hold off an entire squadron armed to the teeth. The
star-riddled night encouraged this spirit of adventure, but these
two cutthroats were too down-to-earth to rhapsodize about the
universe whose enormity would drive them mad if they ever
dared to contemplate its dimensions. They only relied on their
highly active reptilian brains, rarely on the other lobes that func-
tioned stingily at best since they were almost never asked to
do much of anything. And so these two men felt perfectly content. They weren't men who racked their brains or shed light on
this or that subject or aimed to resolve some ancient mystery.
No, their intelligence lay in their ability to scheme. This was all
they needed to survive and outsmart the endeavors of whoever
wasn't on their side.

The mountain worried them as much as it worried the rocks
studding the landscape. On it, they found all they needed to
eat and drink, had strange and entertaining run-ins, and fleeced
plenty of scallywags whose sloppy handiwork had made them
almost rich; they pretended they were criminals being tracked by
the bloodhounds of all the pre-Saharan tribes whom they had,
not long ago, they swore, harassed during their seasonal migra-
tion and from whom they had rustled herds guarded by well-
armed Haratins they'd had no trouble stealthily neutralizing,

strangling them one at a time with an iron wire that left on the throats of its victims a violet mark. "Oh yes," they noted, "we are a walking calamity, a veritable plague of God; woe to those who cross our path! All the tribes of the neighboring desert have heard of our feats and our legend is woven each night around the family hearth. How they fear us, for we do as we wish—we cut down our enemies, rob them blind with impunity, have our way with their daughters and wives and take them if we feel like it. We sell Haratin slaves to the highest bidder, and they better pay up if they want to save themselves from our bad mood because ours could be the last hand to ever touch them."

They came across simple-minded vagrants and ragged transients, and they took pity on them despite the harshness of their hearts. They fed and clothed them cleanly, though they could not relieve them of their discontent nor the lice that had become over time a component of their very being. The Killer and his accomplice were moved by the despair that dogged these beings who'd never asked to be brought into this world and yet found themselves in it with strange, disoriented bodies rejected and despised by the common man, that grunt who gets smashed and bashed and wounded and reviled by thieves and the powers that be and who, in his turn, whales on weaklings, lone women, and animals. And so The Killer and The Butcher sowed havoc in their wake but made amends by helping the most destitute shoulder a little longer their miserable condition.

TWO CUTTHROATS (2)

When they entered Agadir, they saw an airport for the first time and were struck dumb by the way the light sparkled on the wings and fuselages of the airplanes. They had never before been this close to these flying contraptions.

They were totally flabbergasted as they watched these massive, heavy vehicles climb the air without sinking, taking off and landing with terrible rumbles, though they didn't ask themselves too many questions about it, seeing as their brains turned things over slowly and they believed that anything the *roumis* constructed or undertook was the work of the Devil, which seemed even truer based on the incalculable amount of progress made in just a couple centuries of fratricidal war and unbridled scientific innovation. "They've tamed the sea, conquered innumerable distant lands, subdued every sort of rebellious people, and mastered electricity and wind, while the Arabs keep on plowing their way back to the Middle Ages. But we are, like barbarians, full of ourselves and brimming with hate. We'd rather have conflict and crime than good sense and friendship . . . and lo and behold the *roumis* have come once again to inflict on us the iron law of a world that rejects us because it doesn't understand us; but it will still end up overcoming our leeriness and the repulsion that makes a spectacle out of these things we don't understand." So thought The Killer in these moments of clarity and only when pessimism caught hold of him, because in general he didn't have such precise feelings about things; he bobbed along in the tide of the priorities that ordered existence and never complained, knowing that to do so was to risk thwarting the moment, which is to say Fate. In this regard, he was as superstitious and reactive as the gods of Olympus, who were capable of the most unimaginable wickedness but who nonetheless trembled before Fate, the true ruler of the Universe.

They stayed a long time leaning on the white concrete slats of the wall around the airport. They were almost hypnotized by these clockwork birds and even more dazzled by the bearing of the pilots in their regalia who were flitting enigmatically about. Because most of them bore a large sidearm, they concluded that they were soldiers. Which was the case, more or less. They were all over the place. The South had not yet been entirely pacified and most of the mountainous tribes had not accepted that they'd come to impose an order that had little to do with their way of doing things. This was one of the obstacles that had prevented the protectorate from establishing itself even as it locked Morocco in a stranglehold. They'd needed first to convince the various chieftains of a French benevolence that had no intention of changing the habits and customs of the djebel dwellers. They would respect ancestral laws, though the Hakem, which is to say the captain of the French army, would be the one now overseeing all civil functions. He would be advised, of course, by many cadis.

He would conduct justice on behalf, then, of the Makhzen in complete fairness. It would be arranged so that the contradictory sides of this two-headed system of justice would find harmony, but the mountains hadn't yet fully bought in. Chaos still reigned everywhere, and only people like The Killer and The Butcher were able to navigate it as they pleased.

They entered Agadir without much fanfare after having meticulously obscured their weapons under their heaps of motley objects and fabrics. They weren't going to stay in the new sector of town, since no natives were allowed to in those days, but in Talbordjt, a working-class neighborhood built on a hill that overlooked the highway and the port.

Every kind of business was transacted here, which suited them well, since they had no small amount of things to move and other transactions to complete. They found rooms at an inn run by a black keeper; it was spacious and boasted a kitchen that specialized in southern tagines you had to order a day in advance. They were shown to a room without any furniture save a large bulrush mat with two military blankets—not a pillow in sight. In a corner there was a gurglet and an earthen jug. It was still lit by candlelight or gas lamp because electricity had only been run out to the European city and the port. Their new digs suited them perfectly, except for the waves of bedbugs that rushed them as soon as the lights went out. These tiny creatures, none bigger than a lentil, suck the blood of sleepers. They work their way into everything—into the hem of your pants or the holes in your wall or the grooves and gaps in the woodwork. They only come out at night to attack in dense clusters the delicate flesh of men. Eventually the two men complained, and the innkeeper began fumigating immediately. They found small dark corpses all over the packed-earth floor and swept them up gently. From then on, The Killer and his accomplice were no longer woken by or itchy from the bugs' miniscule jaws.

While The Killer haggled with smugglers, The Butcher strutted around the quiet neighborhood, guzzling bottles of beer and wine, fornicating copiously, and coming home only after he'd emptied his sack. He was generally drunk, but he was steady on his legs. Anyone who bumped into or cursed him could expect his worst. The Butcher's intoxication was just a facade—his body was ready at the drop of a hat to strike like a wolf trap. This big swine, whom some might take for a fool, inspired nothing less than an unspeakable fear in those who tried to see him from every angle; only the prostitutes could succeed in taming him for a moment once he'd gone docile in the enchanting grip of the fig brandy and expert touches of these courtesans. Instead of one he'd sleep with many, which considerably increased the strain on their daily finances. But The Killer didn't take much exception to this. He knew The Butcher was sex-crazed; he'd even seen him screw his own mule behind a bush to which he'd tied the animal. And since the mule hadn't seemed to object, and even seemed to display some ebullience thereafter, The Killer concluded that the mule had grown accustomed to this routine.

In those days, zoophilia was common. It had nothing to do with fashion or snobbery. It had no connection whatsoever to some kind of sexual liberation or moral revolution. It happened merely because of the lack of a partner of the same species. Women were the property of the most powerful, and there were few who were able or willing to sleep around without exposing themselves to reprisals. Only people like The Killer had the

audacity to rape women who were otherwise apparently pro-
tected, because no one would take the risk of picking a fight
with this assassin whom nothing, not even death, could deter.

Talbordjt had been the first center of the city, the medina
where Jews and Muslims lived side by side. It was laced with
narrow alleys that were much less cramped than those of the
old centers of Fez or Taroudant. Here, you could move around
with ease. Only heavy trucks couldn't make use of the roads because every turn would prove to be impossible. A large asphalt
street led to a large square where cars and trucks on their way
to Tafraout, Tiznit, or some even more distant destination were
parked. The square was always teeming with people, a mixed
crowd whose cacophony recalled the *moussems* of the South.
There were merchants selling dates, spices, fabric; there were water sellers known as *guerrabs* who frantically shook their leather
handbells; there were storytellers, fortune tellers, auctioneers
hawking Atlassian apes, crafty but easily tamed little monkeys,
censers burning benzoin and incense, writers stationed on their
mats with paper, pen, and inkpot, Saharan druggists armed with
the traditional pharmacopoeia and its plant- and animal-based
materials, concocting natural remedies they sold as antidotes for
snake bites and scorpion stings. They knew how to measure out
potions that could, through inattention, easily become lethal.
This is why it was necessary to measure the dosage based on the
guilty snake or spider. It had to correspond to the deadliness of
the venom. In those days, lots of people perished for lack of an
antidote. The venom of a viper is less potent than a cobra's, and
only a Saharan druggist knows how to prescribe the proper dose
to neutralize each; but because more often than not the victims
didn't know the species of the snake that bit them, sometimes
there was nothing to be done. Even then, though, they would
still take an antidote, just in case.

The square was, like every square in any Arab city, full of a
cheerful heterogeneity, almost carefree, but in league with the
Devil. It was where the most important exchanges took place.
The Killer learned quickly who was there each day so he could
sell his plunder to the highest bidder. He ended up finding an
old Jew who was interested straightaway in his offers and even
more so in his goods. The appearance of this old Jew from

Agadir reminded The Killer of the one in the mountains he and The Butcher had robbed and whose young daughter they'd viciously raped right before the aghast eyes of her parents.

"Do you happen to have a brother in the mountains down south?" The Killer asked.

"No brother, but I do have an uncle. Is it possible you know him?"

"Not really. I've only ever seen him the once."

"I don't see him all that much either. He doesn't come to the city very often, old as he is and not inclined to travel, and I don't go down to the mountains much either—they're lousy with killers and thieves."

"Whoever told you that," The Killer said, "I'll fight to the death."

With that they both burst out laughing.

"We're all thieves," the old Jew said.

"Is that right?"

"You see, I'm not like those other Jews who are scared of their own shadow, who live in squalor and disgrace. I don't take insults lightly. I've beaten up so many thugs who've cursed me or spit in my face. And the cadi bore me out."

"Jews are men just like any other," The Killer said. "Whoever injures or persecutes them ought to be severely punished, because they are people of the Book, just like Christians and Muslims."

From that day forward, he was the friend of that energetic Jew whose drive, guts, and wits he admired. Together they made all sorts of great deals, and The Killer was invited for dinner at the home of his new accomplice on several nights.

The Killer didn't share the same sudden intimacy of his friend, though, because he felt as if he'd just sat down on burning coals; he was worried about the day when his friend would finally glimpse his true nature, and he couldn't allow himself to lose this dealer who had helped him grow his fortune to such ample proportions. So he decided to pay a visit to the uncle in the mountains who now had to disappear: "He must, under no circumstances, ever speak to his nephew about me. The best thing would be to eliminate him, him and his wife. Their daughter, well, we'll have to see . . ." And so it was decided: he would kill

the old man and his wife. This didn't disturb his moral code, because it was just a formality—he had no particular feeling about
it. He was like one of those big beasts of the jungle that imposed
their size and strength on the other animals; he had no scruples,
never woke up in a start, sweating in the grip of an exceptional
terror that rose out of the ruins of the Ten Commandments.
Nope. He was this spotless, nearly impersonal machine that
could snuff out a life just as easily with a bullet or a blade without experiencing a single twinge. At the end of the day, it was a
job like any other. And so he never took into account those mor-
bid details that could cause considerable damage to his psyche,
nor did he use his powers of reflection to do more than land low
blows that he plotted out ingeniously and in the strictest silence.
He was only pleased once the operations had a good chance of
succeeding, which was generally what happened since he never
left anything to chance. He was as meticulous as an orb weaver
spider and as fixed in his desire to harm his enemies as a devil
from the sinister depths of the Hebraic Gehenna. Which is why
he was always quick, whenever it was necessary, to create a void
around himself. He often felt as if he were acting inside an immense ring that nothing else could enter. Others considered him
a living legend, and many a troubadour had sung of his deeds
to the accompaniment of a *lotar* or a *guembri,* which made him
smile, given that these deeds were nothing more than crimes
committed under the seal of an authority stamped upon him
by widespread spinelessness. Several *fquihs,* though, denounced
him at no risk to themselves, because they were unaware that
this rat had, beneath its apparently impenetrable hide, a soul
sensitive to the mysteries of the Beyond. For his part, he thought
of the *fquihs* as simpletons with whom he should never, under any circumstances, pick a fight. Their diatribes or jeremiads
didn't, for him, have any teeth: "At the end of the day, I'm the
one who calls the shots around here, not them, even if they're
brimming with dangerous occult powers."

A little while after their quiet arrival in this port city, which
they had visited before only in dreams, The Killer, who had
kept a low profile in order to escape notice, was summoned to
the city's central barracks, where he was to meet with a colonel
in the French army, one known as Officer Chleuh, since he'd

mastered the Berber language of the Souss and the pre-Saharan hinterlands. This famous colonel was none other than the celebrated Colonel Justinard, who had conducted highly commended research on the Berber tribes and who had produced magisterial translations of Chleuh poems. He'd also taken an interest in the House of Illigh and other chiefdoms. He recorded all of his labors in books that, as it happens, are superbly well written. As soon as The Killer and the friendly officer met, they struck up a frank and lively conversation.

"Sidi Hmad," the officer said, "we have heard a lot about you. Your reputation for bravery and order has earned you admirers around here. We've summoned you here to request your assistance in pacifying the mountains. We have chosen you because you're one of the most powerful chiefs in the Adrar. The man able to resist your striking arguments hasn't yet been born, it's been said."

They both laughed.

"Naturally," the colonel resumed, "we would like to name you the Amghar of your region. Unless you were hoping for the whole *caïdat,* in which case we could be amenable."

"My dear colonel, what France proposes sadly exceeds my abilities. I am merely a fighter, not an administrator, and in my role as chief of my little backwater, I maintain a mere semblance of order, seeing as everyone is well armed with both weapons and reasons to tear each other apart. I'm feared, but only because I'm a crack shot—I don't hold any real power over my peers. They'd snap my neck at the slightest misstep, which is why I'm always on my toes."

"I think you're mistaken about the extent of your power, Sidi Hmad," the colonel replied. "You are very feared, but also highly respected. Your word is worth its weight in gold. You could become quite the agent for the Makhzen and for France. We would be very grateful to you. And our gratitude pays."

"Well, having thought about it, my mind is made up. I'll do it," The Killer responded. "But what will I be expected to do?"

"To begin with, you'll need to pay off the imams so they'll quit prophesying against France and the Sultan during Friday prayers. Everyone knows every man of the cloth is crooked, whatever his stripe. Then, you'll need to bribe the more reluctant bigwigs. That way, our incursion will pose no danger to the people. If some loony objects, though, we'll be forced to use our planes, infantry, and heavy artillery. It should be clear that France seeks to establish peace, prosperity, and education in these places where, right now, anarchy, ignorance, misery, and death are in power. It's vital that you succeed in persuading your people that France is on their side and will be a guardian who will bring them all the benefits of modern civilization. As a matter of fact, France has the money, the teachers, simply put, the men and women who will work hard to pull this nation out of darkness and anarchy. It's already happening in the north, where we've built new cities, dug ports, paved roads and laid train tracks."

"Train tracks? What are those?" The Killer asked.

"Train tracks are metal rails. For trains to run on."

"Trains?" The Killer was confused. He'd never heard anyone talk about this before.

"Right, a train is a group of cars linked together to an engine which pulls them along behind it. It's also called a locomotive."

"I still don't understand," The Killer said.

The colonel pulled a photo album from a shelf. Then he showed The Killer photographs and etchings depicting stations and trains.

"I've never seen anything like that!" The Killer exclaimed. "To think that here, it's the horseshit-powered engine that drives everything and has since antiquity. If France makes all her riches available to us, then you must have designs on the Sherifian Empire."

"Designs, yes, but designs that intend to respect the empire's sovereignty, habits and customs, religion, and law. In fact, we're here to emancipate the Moroccan people. One day or another, though, we will have to step aside. At least that is what Marshal Lyautey has taught us; he loved Morocco so much he considered it his second homeland."

"Hot damn," The Killer enthused. "I'm your guy."

The colonel issued him new guns and fresh ammo, then guided him to the supply office, where he received a large sum of money as an advance against future spending. They then went

to fire the guns in a closed courtyard with fixed targets. The
Killer immediately mastered them. One was a high-precision
machine gun. The Killer was nearly giddy. When they were taking their leave, the colonel had one last thing to say.

"Your friend, what's his name again? Oh, right, The Butcher.
He was detained at a whorehouse where he was giving some
pimp a good beating. He would have killed him, too, if it weren't
for the quick intervention of a squad of *Mokhzanis* who had
quite a time calming your furious friend down. The cadi plans
to sentence him harshly, not for having worked over the pimp
but for being drunk in public. Sharia is unambiguous on this."

"Well, I can't exactly abandon him to this place, let alone in
jail. And as it happens, I'll need him for this new assignment.
You'll need to get him released as soon as you can," The Killer
said.

"You'll have to find a way to motivate the cadi's men."

"I imagine you have better means for that."

"Certainly, I do. I'll get him released. A little baksheesh
should do the trick. He'll be out of the clink in an hour or two,
but try to get him to scram right away; he's a public nuisance.
Sure as sunshine he's got bats in the belfry."

"Bats in the belfry, ha!" The Killer laughed. "He's totally
rung! He's a complete psychopath, fit to be tied, and a vam-
pire to boot. Blood draws him out like a leech from the reeds.
Don't worry, though, we'll be out of this town as soon as you
get him free."

"I'm not finished," the colonel said. "Since you are now one
of us, we thought it would be appropriate that you draw your
salary from the administrative register like any good bureau-
crat faithful to France and the Makhzen. Feel free to collect
whatever amount of money you may need. You can get it from
the supply office and you don't need to justify your expenses.
It comes from a slush fund dedicated to modifying the politics
of reluctant mountain men. You will also need to come to the
barracks monthly and make a report. Unless you'd rather I send
someone to you?"

"No need to send anyone my way. I'll make my report in
person each month," The Killer said.

"Inshallah! I think we're going to be fast friends, Sidi Hmad."

"Without a doubt," The Killer responded.

And with that he was off, driving his heavily laden pack mule before him.

Less than a year later, the French army had pacified a good stretch of the mountains that had till then been restive. But they'd had to use planes, which had created considerable, sometimes gratuitous, damage, because they bombarded instead of fighters souks, homes, and mosques. In any case, the *caïds* ended up signing a surrender, as the mountainfolk had long been subjected to The Killer's persuasive arguments. Those who didn't want to listen to reason were quickly dispatched with the help of a pistol or a poison. They were never spoken of again, and the fence-sitters eventually found themselves on the side of the strongest. France broke trails, built offices, clinics, and schools, and compelled people to allow their children to be taught. Childhood illnesses declined, thanks to French doctors and medicines. Never-before-seen goods flooded the souks. However, a couple of elders succeeded in convincing certain *patresfamilias* to not send their male progeny to the French schools because, as they said, more or less, "They'll turn them into total *roumis,* and then they'll marry infidels, and do you know what that would mean? No? I'll tell you—it would mean the end of the world." Those who had been convinced of the necessity of education sent their sons to school—their daughters weren't allowed and thus weren't required—and those who had not been convinced sent them to the northern cities, where they apprenticed to grocers. In no time at all, things and even mentalities changed under the yoke of the captains in charge of the Atlassian spheres. Crime had for the first time in a long time become a minor concern; only a couple incompetents committed petty larcenies punishable by beatings. It was possible again to travel without fear, because the French army had disarmed everyone besides its recognized agents, among them The Killer, who inspired respect due to the new qualities bestowed upon him by his position in the colonial administration and the Makhzen. His accomplice, The Butcher, returned to slaughtering cows, sheep, and goats. He rose to be the uncontested head of the co-op, but in his gaze there remained a spark as bright and angled as the blade of a whetted cleaver.

Other cutthroats met grislier ends, having impetuously resisted French intrusion. This had signed their death notice, not that they'd known that until it was too late.

THE FISHERMAN AND THE OCEAN

For Professor Brahim Gueddari

The ocean is your close friend; whether it's raging or still, you hunker down on the rock bristling with sharp surf, your rod wedged in a hole made for precisely this purpose, the nylon taut and the tip joggling along to the swell's rhythm.

Elsewhere, you flee as soon as the stupid materialist masses start their jabbering, but here, your patience is infinite.

Here, you are both master of and servant to the elements, which you read and comprehend better than the deafening, convoluted language of the frantic town.

You can read the slightest wrinkle pleating the surface of the sea, which, seen from above, resembles the hide of a full-grown elephant, and your practiced eye deciphers the tern's flight and the gull's dive as it relieves the puffin, just surfacing, of its wriggling prey.

There's no place in your heart for this old thief, whom you curse whenever it lashes out at a bird less crafty than itself.

Whenever a storm pounds the coast, you pass the hours being soaked by spindrift blown in off the open sea, soaking, as it were, in nature's powers released by a monumental undulation nearly as large as the most violent seismic waves.

You find yourself thinking then about the fate of those rockfish who are so often exiled from their home by an unexpected wave. Woe to the fish who hasn't found shelter in time! So often it finds itself, once the water settles, in a shallow puddle where it will be plucked by one of those early-rising beachcombers who scour the shore.

Your fecund imagination fathoms abysses, but instead of the tenebrous darkness of the depths you prefer the comforting appearance of the surface, where beings as diverse as man, bird, and certain fish abide side by side.

Many a time you've reeled in a mullet or sea bass slicked in oil and you've cursed the poorly managed march of technological progress, and whenever the media wheels their cameras over to some major ecological disaster, you brood anew over thoughts of terrible vengeance for those responsible.

Because you know that at this pace, pollution will end up strangling the ocean that so many use like a trash can able to break everything down. They don't know that it's alive, a living environment critical for the survival of the earth.

Of course, this kind of criminality is barely even punished with a short-lived scolding. The hypocrisy fills you with shame and bitterness, you, an ordinary fisherman who only wants the ocean to be as clean as it was when the world began.

THE GRANDFATHER

For Zohour Alaoui

Where two ancient roads cross, there is a burial mound crowned with hundred-year-old junipers;

A blue bird has built its nest there and it warbles at midnight to welcome the Grandfather of vanished peoples . . .

The Grandfather wakes from a stupor that's neither Death as it is in the Bible nor the Dream as it haunts Homer, but some intermediary state;

He shoves away the stone slab that seals his grave and grabs his bow and quiver, stepping into the night like a live flame;

Nocturnal animals—jackals, foxes, owls, and bats—pause their hunting in order to observe this strange being who to them is neither human nor animal, who shimmers diaphanous as a droplet clinging to the web of a spider after the flood . . .

The blue bird who woke the ageless old man has now evaporated into the Cosmos. It will only build its nest now in pock-marked ruins where the clamor of warring tribes harry it.

The Grandfather has crossed deserts and cities, he has haunted old harbors that remind him of nothing because back in his day sailing had not begun;

He becomes a filthy beggar without a bowl and sits himself down on the sticky pavement so he can better admire the bobbing hulls and the bawdy hustle of the fishermen;

Once he oversaw the entirety of the known World and now he'd be happy to spend a lifetime inhaling with enjoyment the port's effluvia and the heady odors of nautical waste.

Then, the overwhelming desire to treat himself to a celebration in the agate palace of Poseidon seizes his mind—and he sees himself surrounded by beautiful nereids dancing a ballet with harlequin triggerfish and honey toads . . .

But he can't swallow anything, because he is a vapor;

He can only feel the unusual burst of an aroma or the smooth whiff of a forbidden dish.

Poor Grandfather, condemned to suffer without reacting to the myriad insults of time.

CITIES

For my friend Moulay Driss Aloui Ismaïli

Nine times destroyed and nine times rebuilt on top of the same ruin, here is the famous Ilium of Homer, Troy, which withstood so much Hellenic Barbarism. Here are Paris and Helen, robed in stupor and radiating love, much to the chagrin of the Olympic gods who were jealous of the happiness of men ready to bribe the inscrutable sky. Here is a city girt with thick ramparts, a city so impregnable only the cunning of Ulysses could topple it. Troy! Restorative blood of the world. From your stone was Aeneas the magician born, founder of Roman might, biological father of Legions and Empire.

A tragic city that knew only the racket of the sword and the marauding fire of an enemy who came from the steep coasts of a sea bristling with islands, a horror for the novice mariner and a glory for the Phaeacians, skilled drivers of tides.

You predicted for us the ruins of the future: of London and Berlin, of Agadir and Al Asnam; the former thanks to the hands of men, the latter to the tectonic might of the Globe, the seismicity essential for the evolution of beings and things.

It is one of the ancient cities still shuddering with the breath of revolutions; those cities whose cobblestones sing of the smoking martyrological blood, spilled by the Church or the inquisitorial butcher; one of those inhuman cities whose outcasts drown it in fire and blood when injustice is raised up to dogma and when misery and drugs plague aimless adolescences, transforming it into an enraged infernal machine; but here and there rise serene cities, white as a dove, carefree and magnificent: Essaouira, Loctudy . . .

Here, the artist can find their footing and let their magic loose . . .

These simple cities know no stress or brutal unrest; they avoid the accelerated history of those centers where the fate of the world is decided in offices as airtight as sarcophagi.

Essaouira, jewel of the South; you still buzz with Phoenician rumors, and your island, riddled once with the workshops of dyers who clothed ancient princes in purple, is home now to the peregrine falcon, that other lord of legend that the biped wields like a weapon against small prey.

But your prey, dear poet, are those scattered images that you bring together into a cosmic symphony.

THE ARGAN TREE

For the doctor and friend Methqal

Venerable, mystical tree, your roots bore through rocks and seal an unsunderable pact with the earth;

you are the hardiest and without a doubt the handsomest example of vegetation;

We'll never know your true age or whether you're the off-spring of some ancient comet;

you blanket the mountainous slopes with an inimitable splendor—you are powerful and able to withstand the raids of goats and crickets who strip you of those leaves that look like emerald shards when the sun exhales with an inaudible murmur its prismatic rainbow-tinted wave;

an unforgettable language springs from your fibers and branches where the palm-nut rat gathers amber nuts it will bury so you will carry on beyond infinity; you defy time, bad weather, heat waves, and the hand of man.

Unchallenged master of the South, you're called Argan but no one knows your true name; maybe the dry wadi knows it, who speaks to the pink laurel with the same gravity of your dark finery;

The grasshopper and the turtledove, unmoved by earthly technicalities, sing of your beauty because you remove them from danger with your impenetrable foliage;

The guest who dwells in the crook of your exposed roots is the solitary cobra whose shrill whistle tunes the fugitive clarity of diurnal dreams;

in summer as in winter, your shadow extends all the way to the foothills as if to inform the mountain goat of a brutal oncoming death;

—the hunter who uprooted you en masse in order to build his dream palace where you'd abided since the time of Noah has fallen from the mountain, struck by a horrible vengeance;—

it is written that whoever scratches you risks telluric lightning;

but you are not the vindictive god who crushes armies in a blinding flash;

inside you the pure Spirit of unknown vastnesses stirs and each of the sky's capital letters is a dazzling star that regales you with the story of the fundamental Chaos;

the Elders called you protective Genie, guardian of men and beasts;

they loved and revered you, whoever consumed the fragrant red oil your bitter almond secretes when summer reaches its zenith;

o tree tougher than granite and agate, no whirlwind or *chergui* can dismember your crown;

young or old, twisted or slim, you enhalo the scree with an aura only anchorites can see;

at the bottom of wells and in the troglodyte's throat, your immaterial essence trembles;

your idiom scrawled in the holy grimoires that shield the blue scarab from the beams of mythical gems;

old Argan, I greet you from the depths of a world that only knows you through the cosmetics pressed from your elliptical almond.

TWO GHOULS

For Hassan Abouyoub, M'Hamed's son

No sooner had they stepped out of the deep shadows did one start barking ferociously (radio waves bothered him) while the other, wearing an iron muzzle, stumbled, because he couldn't see a damned thing for all the blue of this day the likes of which he'd never seen. Like iguanas, they were both trying to move forward, but their enormous shadow frightened them. It was standing straight up, instead of spreading out or hugging the contours of the terrain; it repeated the wild gestures they were making even as they terrified them.

The shadow must be a trap for them, they thought. They wondered who, exactly, they were, where they'd come from, but they came up empty; whoever passed by them didn't see them. They had washed up in a world where they had no substance. But this land reminded them of something. However, because they couldn't distinguish what was and what was not—and what counted as a physical body—doubt crept in and gnawed away at them with such intensity that they viewed everything around them only crudely. They were worse off than if they hadn't seen or understood anything at all of what was unfolding around them in this world to which they'd been sent by some entity for disciplinary reasons: a supreme punishment that the metalloid gods inflicted upon volcanoes and their various adjuncts: fumaroles and geysers and other infernal openings that cause the lithosphere so much incredible damage.

But The Muzzle and The Barker were just a couple of minions; they hadn't shown a sufficient amount of respect for Satan, master of calamities and conflagrations . . .

They had stolen the golden crutches of Hephaestus, patron saint of holy smithies . . .

And so they had been sent here for a fitting reeducation. Even if it meant that they became blind nomads, even poltergeists, they had to wander and wander ceaselessly until some distant voice surged from out of nowhere to put them back on the path; sooner or later they'd return home, to that excruciating inferno and its wild vapors.

Their wandering went on a long time. Though when they had to stop for a bit, they had no problem slipping into some mountain village where they were accepted right away. They weren't dummies, these two rogues, and they had plenty of resources.

Eventually they found the body of a man, which they then polished up until they were able to approach the rustic folk they'd been rubbing shoulders with.

We are saints, they told the villagers. We will stay with you and as long as we do, you will prosper. However, the day will come when we will disappear as suddenly as we arrived. We are no more than shadows.

As soon as the peroration ended, the villagers sacrificed seven goats and erected a sandstone wall against bad luck.

That night a rabid dog was buried after having died at the unbitten hands of various urchins who had dispatched it with sharp stones. An old black woman was also buried—they said she brewed magic potions and crafted amulets, sometimes using the genitals of female porcupines in order to bewitch wayward men. She perished thanks to the careful attention of The Muzzle, whose metal muzzle The Barker had removed. And so they feasted and sang until dawn.

The ghouls were coming to enjoy this simple little world where not even the slightest explosion or conflict erupted. A clergyman murmuring verses he didn't understand came to greet them. He wanted to honor them, for in his eyes they were two archangels come from the remote heavens, heavens to which the masses could not ascend. They allowed themselves to be buffeted by his paltry panegyric. Beautiful girls danced in homage to them, spinning around like angry wasps and in intricate rounds undergirded by frantic musical swells that pricked the senses before giving way to the calm that precedes grand banquets.

An oven-roasted goat was served to the ghouls, but seeing as they were nothing more than corporeal apparitions, they had to dissolve the carcass mentally. Murmuring ran through the crowd: "What tremendous appetites!" "They could swallow us whole!"

The village chief, one of those leathery old bastards whom nothing surprised because his motto was "God is God Alone but, after him, I'm in charge here," this chief saw the two saints, tried to fix them in his shark-like memory with an intensity bordering on violence and defilement, and all the worse for him. He was immediately smote. On the double they took up his remains, but two black men, his henchmen, took charge of the body, dug a hole and buried it. No one objected—the henchmen would have strangled anyone foolish enough to protest. Everyone wept. Dogs went to sniff around the burial mound and ran off quick. A man in the crowd broke the silence: "Look! Everyone, look! The Saints are with us. The one in charge is no more but the Saints remain!"

The grave was staked with spiny branches to keep scavengers from digging up the corpse. The Saints said, "Henchmen, you've just committed a sacrilege. You've buried a living man! And for no reason! He isn't dead. A curse upon you both!" The two henchmen ran for the hills, but they were caught immediately and put before the Saints for judgment.

"Put them to death!" the ghouls pronounced.

And they were executed on the spot.

A flutist blew into his instrument. He had the red eyes of someone who regularly partook of too much kif and *mahia*. The blaze that lit the scene crackled. In the middle of the square, strange shapes yielded to other strange shapes on the black screen of night, which trembled and seemed transitory. This was the appearance of a stick-thin world that burned like a candlewick. Muffled steps, thuds, stifled sighs, and then a sudden cry: "Throw them to the carrion birds!"

"No," the Saints said. "We want their skin. It is so lustrous. Bring it to us."

The two henchmen were flayed and their skins brought to the Saints.

"You see," the ghouls said, "you have paid homage to us now. We will bring these skins with us. In fact, we must leave now. We are only here for a moment; you must now return to your own fates, though we shall watch over you wherever we are. We have already almost departed.

"Be vigilant. Your children will only recognize you when you have been for them a reliable mirror, the mirror of the Universe. We will always be with you, for we love you. One day, you will leave this village to move among the world. Your houses will fall into ruin. You will become rich and sophisticated; your material and mental misery will cease. But you will encounter other miseries. Miseries more fatal than hunger. Nevertheless, you will overcome these disasters. You will survive murders and the worst humiliations. Go, and live!"

With this, the Saints dissolved into the shadows of the sky. They became invisible again even though they were still there.

"It's been millions of years now that I've been following you in your rambles," The Muzzle said. "Why do I have to keep wearing this dog skin?"

"The better to see you in your true trappings," The Barker responded.

"But I don't need anything!"

"Just do it! We've been exiled to a world that knows nothing about us. A world made of predation, corruption, murders, and everything in between. I don't know why I'm here on some special mission, but I have to act and take care of things! Obviously I made some kind of mistake along the way. It's been a long time since I've remembered anything. What can we do? One mistake made here is worth ten times worse."

"No need to go into details," a voice from beyond the grave said. "Respect what you see around you and even more importantly what you hear. You will remain here for some time, but you will start again someday at square one."

"Finally! I haven't been forgotten!"

They crossed fizzing deserts, survived wars among brothers and nations, dressed themselves in chaos, participated in genocides and helped out in enormous massacres. Shells of every caliber, bullets and madnesses pierced them. They felt no pain at all because they were made of air. They were assailed by the homilies of carnival prophets they thought of as babbling.

After all these displays, they saw entire swaths of humanity drop. Debauchery was going strong; the pillaging was legendary. They watched rough creatures butcher children to grill and devour them with delight. Like common piglets. And extravagant prostitutes, and luxurious pederasts. Reckless insanity. They sent to the Supreme Master this laconic message:

"We are here. The land is beautiful. There is fighting. Everything is ready to be remade. We await your orders."

It was time to call them back. "They did exactly as they were told. Put them back in the game!"

"What an impossible task, this wandering," they said. "Thank goodness we'll return home someday. What a nightmare this world is."

And up on high, this poor world had been entirely forgotten.

SEEN FROM THE CANOPY

The primordial forest never sleeps; it hums and breathes with the warm, humid rhythm of ancient growth.

The number of microscopic creatures living and breeding in this lush horticultural jumble which the masses call virgin forest cannot by anyone be counted.

The only way to move through it is with a machete's help, working your way around obstacles and venomous snakes that the untrained eye might mistake for thin vines or green branches.

This ageless Amazon conceals treasures no Ali Baba could even dream of. Gold is omnipresent; it glitters in the alluvial silt of rivers, driving the white prospector mad when he's not hunting with his rifle the Indians his plentiful diseases have not yet blessed.

In order to corrupt the Indian, the wily, avaricious prospector introduces him to alcohol and tobacco. The fiend burns down the forest so he can more easily dig up the subsoil. He pours huge quantities of mercury into the river so it will draw the gold flakes into lumps, poisoning in the process the aquatic flora and fauna and, at the other end of the food chain, the Indian who only knows how to live by hunting, gathering, and fishing. This disastrous creature, this despicable prospector, drags his rake through the untouched world where animal, insect, plant, and Indian have lived in symbiotic balance before his destabilizing invasion.

Wherever he goes, he builds dissonant shacks in the otherwise harmonious bucolic landscape: brothels and gambling parlors flourish in these places where the only reliable thing is your revolver.

This is the Wild West of Brazil, where the acrid scent of gunpowder has replaced the sweetness of sugar. A Wild West where single combat rarely happens.

Plenty of explorers have set off with their heads brimming with magnificent ideas, only to find themselves six feet underground. Pimps and bootleggers are the only ones who win this deadly game. They're the only ones who run no risk in gathering the gold these surveyors, hypnotized by an untouchable bonanza, have maimed and killed for.

The Indian flees through the silence of the canopy, dreading this invading anarchy as if it were an army of demons. He plunges deep into the leafy mass which he respects like a mother, a shelter, and a future grave. He knows that one day his body will nourish the essence of the warm, steaming humus. This is how he wanders through this otherworldly universe, where every creature is different from the other.

THE ASYLUM

For my friend the professor Jidal Bouchaïb

"Not much worse than separation," a man, alone, says out loud. Behind him a windmill creaks, and around him, the countryside is dry and reddish; only argan, date, and cedar trees cut through the general monotony. From time to time, there's the cry of a crested lark; of the jay they call the "hajji of birds"; and, intermittently, the rustle of a snake hunting gray squirrels. The man gazes at the large door of the building that overlooks the road and the cemetery. He shivers as if struck by a magnetic wave. "I wouldn't want to be shut up in there," he says. "Better to be dead!" All sorts of shouts, yelps, demands, countermands, prayers, and insults emanate from within. The asylum for the mad (for it really is an asylum for mental patients) rattles but doesn't burst. Whoever sees the madmen who live there would know, though, that those within are wiser than those without. There are no arguments, no fights; there's yelling, of course, yells and prayers sent up to the clear sky, which laughs at this miserable tribe.

The man enters the building.

"I'm a journalist," he tells the guard. "I have been appointed to see what your prisoners need."

"They barely have a thing; we've been completely forgotten. Write that down and say it loud and clear, so that people will know that there are hundreds of needy people, young and old and everything in between, who have been shattered by fate like mirrors for having come too close to clarity."

"Anyone with a clear conscience will be stirred," the journalist replied. "May I take some pictures?"

"By all means."

He photographs a large black man, half-nude and calling everyone to prayer every five minutes, turning toward the west and not toward the Kaaba. This ad hoc muezzin recites the verse ad infinitum. After each call, he sits and begins methodically crushing the fleas and nits infesting his crotch. He seems mesmerized by these arthropods feeding off his blood. Occasionally he takes a red flea and inspects it in the sunlight, then laughs loudly before standing again to start a new call to prayer.

"He's missed his calling," the journalist says.

"Not at all," the guard corrects him. "He actually was a muezzin. But the hippies gave him too strong a dose of LSD. In fact, most of the people here are victims of the hippies. They're the ones who introduced that lethal poison to the Essaouira peninsula. They literally led the urban youth astray. There's a fantastic photographer here who used to live in Sydney, in Australia. He had everything back there: a job, a house, a wife and kids. One day, nostalgia bit him and he came back—even the Jewish diaspora comes back, as a pilgrimage; all the worse for him. The hippies offered him the storied LSD. He took so much he washed up here in the asylum."

"What about the older ones here?" the journalist asks.

"They're not so much crazy as senile. They don't have anything, so we've taken them into our care so they can live out their final days without having to worry about the day to day. You may have noticed they're not speaking. They're listless but not in distress. Sad, yes, though they're sad because a woman they all loved died the other night. They haven't wept, haven't shown any sort of revolt against fate, but they've sunk into total muteness."

He goes on to tell the story of the building.

"Right now we're standing in what used to be an arsenal for the French army. It dates back to at least the time of Marshal Lyautey. It was completely renovated in order to accommodate these poor folks who only have guardian angels for family. If only you knew how much I've suffered to see them with no care, no doctor, no good food or medicine. They've been put here, far from town, so they can be more easily forgotten. People fear the insane, that's why they're placed in quarantine. A prisoner has more rights than they do. You'll say all this in your article, won't you?"

"Will I ever!"

"No one ever comes to see them. The municipality has settled on sending a truck full of food every now and then, but that's it. When anyone falls ill, they're made comfortable, but if their condition worsens, they wait calmly for death because they know they're already dead in the eyes of their peers."

At that moment, two disheveled young women run out of their area and accost the journalist, who is smoking a cigarette. They ask him for so many he ends up giving them his whole pack.

"They smoke," he says.

"Yep, they were prostitutes before. They have a weakness for tobacco. You see how they're gone now—happy to have an unexpected present. Soon enough they'll sing your praises; they'll bless you in their way. Prayers that come from creatures as pure as they are are granted right away by the Most High, bet your bottom dollar."

"Well," the journalist says, "I'll do all I can to get someone to take care of these poor wretches." And with that he leaves the asylum.

Outside, the summer sun beats down on the stones. Only a chorus of cicadas and the distant backfiring of a truck interrupt the luminous silence, which gathers the landscape into its charitable torpor.

THE HOUSE

For Denis Roche

It was a dream, one of those dreams that only comes to us once in a while. The setting was the dwelling of our elders, a very big house with thick stone walls and high balconies pierced with slits from which you could fire, with complete safety, on the bandits who teemed in the region back then like eels in a tank.

Once again, I was dreaming. Dreaming and walking among men and women and children and babies; it must have been a holiday. Or a burial? There I was, alone, walking through the crowd, people packed together, almost stuck, but they couldn't feel or see me—I was there only as a memory. A distant memory, so slight it was like a thin thread ready to snap, release its connection to the original shape, the tapestry and the frame. It had to have been either a joyous holiday or a communal mourning. Lots of comings and goings in our house built on an impressive rock of this mountain of the South graced by so many birds and storms.

I walked among this teeming mass without a clue as to why I was there. Some of them were eating tagines, with chicken, almonds, honey, fermented butter, and couscous cooked in earthen pots, a succulent meal. Others were talking in corners about confidential subjects. There were spinsters, and mothers with babies on their backs. And I was there too. Our old house, the elders', had been transformed into a huge labyrinthine hole. As I made my way around this shifty place, the very place I'd been born, everything vanished. The hallways, the rooms, all became different things. At one point, I found myself at the end of a tunnel guarded by two watchdogs who bounded over when I whistled. The big one, who must have been the male, sat right next to me. I speechified to him for a while and this dog understood everything! He watched me with the astonished, incredulous eyes of a fearless animal who knew it was loved. Beside us was a unfathomable chasm, but the two creatures didn't give two figs. They weren't scared of me, let alone this cliff.

And then I heard a knock. The woman who ran the Balima Hotel shattered the dream by waking me.

These two watchdogs were eminently stoic: they could tear to pieces anyone who happened to cross their path. They weren't emaciated or mangy. Not the kinds of ownerless dogs the police kill every morning. These were mutts who loved man, in whom they saw a natural protector. A brother who called out to them from afar when disaster was headed their way.

I opened the male's muzzle and put my fist in his mouth, to test him. He wagged his tail straight off. Could this really be a dog? There wasn't an ounce of brute in him. There was an expansive universe, instead.

"What a dog," I said.

Just a pup. And he stayed right by me, the female behind him. "What could this dream mean?" I wondered. To try to extract the meaning from it would just end up distorting it. Because it's impossible to see anything clearly in it right now. "I guess we'll see later on," I said.

And I looked over at the unfathomable chasm. And next to me the watchdogs. They were handsome and placid. There was no way they were of this world. They had filled me with such joy.

THE LAST WILL AND TESTAMENT
OF A DYING MAN

What's that? I'm not even half-dead yet but here come all
these scavengers, scrabbling for a crack at my corpse. It's worth
asking myself if I, whom they'd always acted like they were in
awe of, ever inspired them. Whatever the case, there are two
for sure who can't wait to start tearing me apart, that much is
clear. You know, though, I had to let things happen . . . but this
whole thing has gone on too long, much as it may have needed
to, far as I know. I couldn't tell you who was one and who was
the other, that's how much they look like each other, diligently
sporting the mask of some oaf ever so slightly less fearsome
than their accomplices, who are showing off at the wheel of
a late-model Rolls while the masses sag under the weight of a
relentless misery. Not even the builders of these luxury vehicles
drive them, I've heard—they settle just fine for a typical clunker,
it seems. Yep, I let things go, but I had no idea that a flood
would come and sweep away with a flick all that I'd built: the
Constitution, the central party, human rights, a market economy, to name a few. And today, my god, two scroungers are
lying in wait for the slightest shake of the age-worn body my
soul seems long ago to have stepped out of. There they are, like
two beady-eyed vultures, waiting for the final spasm to rack me
so they can tear apart a still-warm corpse. And I can see rising
in the vacant pupils framed by their sleep-heavy lids blood-red
dawns like those that have brought civil war to Liberia, Bosnia,
Angola, Sudan, Somalia, where rampaging soldiers deal directly
with the Devil, the true conductor of this era's disoriented and
frantic orchestra.

"The old man doesn't have much longer," they're thinking,
and in their minds they're already rubbing their hands, savoring
the victory they each think they'll achieve over the other. He's
got a couple hours more, tops . . . a couple days at the most.

And if it comes to pass that he croaks before the problem of succession's been settled, we'll do what we can to hide his death from the insolent gossipmongering press, until such time that things fall into place. Woe to he who hasn't clearly named his heir! Bah. We're not going to make a second Franco out of him. If he dies, fine—he dies. We'll build him a mausoleum where he'll be watched over forever by the spirits of our Elders, far from this former village of thatched huts that over the course of time has become a small European city brimming with amenities and cosmopolitanism. "No doubt in my mind that's what those two are thinking right now," the Old Man said out loud, before a pained whistling escaped his chest. The nurse attending to him immediately recorded in a notebook what the illustrious dying man had said and then got up to sponge his forehead starred with stubborn beads of sweat. She returned to her chair, and as she leafed through an African magazine that reported in great detail on the illness of the patriarch and the dense mystery surrounding it in the eyes of the outside world, she couldn't help but note that this old man was hardier than any young man of twenty years.

"They don't want it getting out, but there's really no doubt that he's on his last legs. It can't be a question of more than a couple hours . . ."

Too many schemes were whirling around this specter lurking in the antechamber of this tidy room where cutting-edge medical devices labored to keep in a quasi-vegetative state an old man who had no desire to leave. An underhanded, ruthless struggle stretched from one day to the next between clans, factions, and other gangs of the presidential elite, each of them striving to grab hold of power before the Elder delivered his soul to God.

Though he was all but underground, the old man continued to keep hold of, by the thinnest thread, a sense of lucidity against all odds; and those who had an intimate knowledge of this little world of hypocrites, braggarts, and upstarts were worried that once he was gone his country would fall prey to anarchy, the wrath of the majority, ethnic strife—in other words all the endemic diseases Africa has incubated in its darkest depths since time immemorial. But any politician as shrewd as this old navigator of History's byways knows, of course, that the fragile balance he'd instituted and that rested solely on his credibility could not survive the constant assaults of time's vicissitudes forever. "Listen! They are hyenas. All that nature in her bounty has created which is evil and most putrid has worked its way into the very gears of the State. Those men have no heart. These poor people—I'm leaving them to a pack of wild dogs that will tear them apart before they even realize it's started! So patiently did I build this country up in the face of headwinds and rogue tides, and in a time when democracy was in shambles, I got the authorities to respect everyone's essential liberties. Everywhere else, people were fighting over seats and forgetting the economy. They all saw me for what I was: a perfect democrat and a wise, steady hand. Today, everyone, even the worst dictators, zip themselves up lickety-split in the good old uniform of democracy and blather about being more democratic than me. So what! They'll get their comeuppance sooner or later where they least expect it. And while certain women in my entourage play at witchcraft and complicate an already reasonably confusing game, others rattle bells that ring as if my passing will usher us out of an ordinary age into a long-hoped-for golden one. How wrong these devils are—they don't realize they're celebrating their own fall from grace. It's true, some ambitious career soldier could pop up like a devil from his box, that kind of thing's possible with that group of poor bastards. A purge like none before it could happen right now and I'd laugh myself silly from the bottom of my little black hole. They're going to miss me and it won't be until that fateful moment that they'll finally understand the meaning of charismatic power, because by then all the good things I brought about will have vanished, leaving this little world of schemers exposed and trembling."

The Old Man understood everything except for where he was—what country or which European city, even what kind of building. His grey matter worked intermittently while his failing body responded weakly to the remedies they were stuffing into it. There were lots of comings and goings around him, always the same ones: some faces were radiant, some were worried. Among the blur there were doctors, too, recognizable by the authority that lent them an uncommon bearing and access, as well as nurses with angelic kindness. Often there was an incomparably beautiful woman, wreathed in a halo studded with stars that sparkled blue and milky as opals. The Old Man wondered who she could be: "Maybe an angel or one of those deceptive apparitions the Devil is so fond of? No, that can't be it, her beauty isn't demonic. She radiates a perfect serenity. If I'm not mistaken, then she must be the mother of our Lord and Savior Jesus Christ." He was not mistaken. This vision was indeed of Mary. She smiled as she offered him her hand, and he could see himself rising as the rags and heavy objects trying to keep him fastened to an invisible platform fell away and he twisted with all his might the hands that were holding him back; then he rose and left behind him the land that was burning his skin. He tried to get nearer to the Virgin whose halo blinded him. She didn't retreat, but he was unable to touch her, as she was merely an intangible image. Thus the Old Man came to understand that he had been chosen by God and that this sudden visitation was the sign that soon he would join the saints and apostles in Paradise.

"And so I shall be finally at peace. Farewell, world, to which I tried to bring a touch of justice and humanity. But what is there to be done, my Lord? Man isn't yet ready to understand the virtues of labor relations, equality, and respecting the other. He prefers cunning, ploys, and clashes. Though the men of to-day are no longer those of yesterday. They seem to run toward their demise because they are greedy and dislike the truth. Just look at how these vultures are mentally feasting on my political shadow! Each of them believes the seat will be theirs, and it's this idea that's pushing them to play a dirty trick on their peers. They're trying to neutralize one another, like Florentines. But even at this moment as I cross the stream, without much difficulty, well, and in spite of the horrible physical agony wrought on me by this fucking cancer that none of the chemicals swirling in me has been able to dam, even as I cross this old river that leads straight to Hades, empire of shadows and Furies, I don't see any celebrations more remarkable than the ones I was in the habit of hosting for the people during my heyday. But my death, or perhaps the beginning of my legend, should be a good opportunity for, not a national period of mourning, but a bounteous festival. That would certainly erase the rivalries, resentments, and gnawing hatreds which are the typical lot of seasoned politicians. I would then be able to enter the other world with the serene soul of a man who truly understood and loved his people, not with the sad image they expect of one at the end of his reign . . ."

Three times a day the one who'd always been thought of as the only likely heir came to ask after the illustrious patient's general condition, an old baron from the previous order who had amassed an enormous fortune he'd stored secretly in Switzerland or elsewhere, one so big that people said, in all seriousness, that he could finance a small civil war between bosom buddies. "But the more they gobble down the more they ask for. Ogres, all of them," the Old Man said to himself. "This pseudo-disciple isn't worth more than any others." As for the others, they didn't think much of what was coming for the Grandfather: "If he's losing his marbles, then he's starting the move. If only he could get a little help to get it over and done with! It's been months now of this agony inching along. But it's impossible—everyone's watching everyone else. You couldn't even pay someone to euthanize him even though he's suffering so awfully. He's clinging to life like a limpet to a rock. He's going to be a pain in the ass to the very end, but whatever. It's just a question of hours, and then his seat will be mine! Good thing the papers are following this so closely. There will be such lovely editorials written when I'm buried, though it won't be so simple as that . . ."

The Old Man saw in blinding flashes images of him being buried while the whole world watched. And then he was rising into a different sky, beyond all the dust and constellations, through a light in which there was nothing but Infinity, the extreme mirror of every risk and every essence.

"They're all saying I'm some old schmuck, a broken relic that needs to be swept away! But when was the last time they took a good look at themselves in the mirror? Nope, nope, their thoughts are as stubborn and unbendable as a spearhead. The criminals! But that's not my problem, I'm already on my way out. They're going to skin each other alive and woe to those who can't keep up! As for me, eternal joy is waiting." These words exploded in his head in full view of the pretenders haunting the room in which he was yanking, left and right, the bridle of Erebus's dark horse.

"But everyone always thinks he's going to find a way out of the pain that's taking him away. But I don't—I don't think he'll be able to slip the force of the current that's dragging him to the chasm from which no one ever returns. It's like the closer he gets to it, though, the more he perks up. It's true many have often seen him as a substitute pope or some kind of saint. Wouldn't that make him a little loony? He even built a basilica that's an exact replica of the Sistine Chapel. A madness of this scope is rare. He never understood that his Catholicism actually bans this kind of counterfeiting, but his senility won out over his good sense. And look at him now, in the sticky grip of the Grim Reaper who recognizes no pope or saint or person. He'll be scythed like a sheaf of dry wheat and everyone will shed a crocodile tear. As for me, as I wait for that final departure I'll act just like the others, wearing my false mask of tragedy to pull the wool over everyone's eyes."

The Old Man wasn't that incapacitated; he had flashes of lucidity and could still tell one person from another by their posture alone. He hadn't yet lost the capacity that had so often allowed him to read the truth each person hid deep inside themselves. And even though his body was unresponsive, his political wit and instincts remained sharp. He was, though, collapsing; the cancer had metastasized severely and had eaten his body away so that it was like the slack hide of a sheep that moth larvae had reduced to a heap of gray dust. And so he was going toward his annihilation without complaint or any concern for the schemes hatching around him. He considered himself outside time, and already his image appeared to him like a halo in a distant sky more spacious and luminous than this edge of the jungle teeming with soldiers and slavering beasts. This father of a nation whom everyone revered sparkled, now, above the masses like a galaxy: he was the final dinosaur of a lost Africa, a holy man on his way toward the kingdom of shadows who only had to walk through the radiant tunnel that cataleptics always described. "Because I don't believe in myths," he whispered with an imperceptible shiver. "God and Jesus are with me and shall be until the end." It seemed to him as if he'd come into this world only for this final apotheosis, which some could only understand as a farce unworthy of a man of his stature. It was, for them, utterly ludicrous. The final proof of his megalomania that had so often been his motto! But those who thought this way were nothing but hypocrites who too swiftly passed over his numerous other qualities, not that this was their primary virtue. No, that would be how they'd rather inflict upon the masses the worst damage and trigger unprecedented bankruptcies, like so many others before them. Such were the people nitpicking the Old Man despite the scant hope that there was among his mob a couple of disciples able to follow his example to the letter. Had he not been a calm and steady hand guiding them along the proper way even as neighboring nations foundered? There might be a possibility of avoiding a terrible outcome, because not everyone is corrupt, not by a long shot! But he knew, too, that only the strong could win out, and those were no altar boys, my goodness. They look to their own interests first—the rest aren't their concern. This was what the renowned and dying man feared the most. He did not want to abandon his flock (which is what he called his constituents) to an orphanage where only the most willful thugs could make the law. "Apres moi, le deluge, so many of my ignorant and unconscionable counterparts have said. But no! After me, I say, comes spring, because I don't despair about human nature. Africa shall wake from this heavy legendary slumber into which it's been sunk for centuries, and I will, of course, be remembered. I will be honored until the extinction of the human race. But have I made a mistake and lost it all by not naming an heir? No! I didn't name one because the Constitution is absolutely clear about that. All they have to do is apply its methods and terms. In any case, they will have to do it this way. We're not Zulus or savages. My people are educated. Possibly ravenous, compulsive, and ambitious, but well educated. They're not going to tear each other apart in order to be the sole one in charge. They will find a way to govern together, on excellent terms, up until elections can be held. As for me, I can leave in peace." He knew, now, that he was back in his homeland. In Europe, they hadn't been able to take proper care of him. The whitecoats (the whitedevils, he thought, smiling deep down) had decreed that the illness had spread to such a degree that it was now entirely incurable. They'd shuttled the poor wretch from one clinic to another like an object they couldn't wait to be rid of, a heavy, cumbersome object. And in order to do this, they'd pumped him full of various drugs so he'd be none the wiser about these rough transfers. Only the doctors were able to make decisions in this regard, though his entourage continued to watch over things and execute orders without hesitation. Today, he was home, in his own residence, at the edge of a virgin forest that hummed with the spirits of the ancestors and whose splendor he had loved so much. He was home, and he felt it. "They wouldn't do this to an old man! Not this! I've come back here to be buried in proverbial privacy. The kind only enjoyed by the apostles, saints, and martyrs of the Church's earliest days . . . I feel no pain, now. I am completely independent from my body even though it continues to keep me here. I can already hear the drums and sobs, the sorcerers' warnings, the speeches and condolences. All the hypocrisy of the world that thinks it's giving me a final dignified sendoff even though they're getting it so wrong. But here they come; I ought to keep my mouth shut. But who's that? Who's there? No one? Maybe it's the evening falling so heavily that I can hear it break itself into a thatchwork of small dark stripes. Or maybe I'm simply hearing the slippered steps of Death. That's it. There it is, inside me, weaving throughout me, gnawing my blood and bones, smiling and glowing, shining out—it doesn't look anything like that crude image we have of it, it's more graceful, attractive even. And there it is—I'm off."

NOTES ON PUBLICATION HISTORY

"The Burial," winner of the Prix de la nouvelle maghrébine, first appeared in *Preuves* 184 (June 1966): 3–8. Two accounts confirm the argument made in the [original] introduction to this story. In an interview from 1974, Khaïr-Eddine stated the following: "Before *Agadir* came out, I had a bit of a reputation. I was publishing with some of the big journals, who put my name on the cover. That's how it went, for example, when I won the Prix de la nouvelle maghrébine, put on by the journal *Preuves*. That gave me my first real boost. One morning, I got a letter telling me that my story "The Burial" had received the prize. I was surprised, because I'd completely forgotten the very existence of the story. But after racking my brains, I remembered having read in a newspaper, in Casablanca, a little notice inviting Maghrebi writers to submit to the Prix de la nouvelle. I remember that I'd sent this story in about a year and a half before, to *Preuves*. I received the prize money when I had nothing to live on, and I couldn't have been more delighted." "Interview with Mohammed Khaïr-Eddine," in *Al Mawkif Al-Adabi* (Damascus), no. 9 (1974): 28–46, with Qusim Al-Chouaf and Annie Khaïr-Eddine.

The second account comes from a friend of the author, the writer and journalist André Laude. In an article titled "Khaïr-Eddine, Tectonic Poet," he wrote: "In 1963, he wrote 'The Burial'; in 1964, he published *Black Nausea*, a slim volume of poems, and he published in *Marginales, Le journal des poètes, Encres vives, Carbone* (Belgium) . . . Now, Paris was celebrating him. Maurice Nadeau, the editor of *Lettres nouvelles,* was about to publish a story of Khaïr-Eddine's. The 'Prix de la nouvelle maghrébine,' created by *Preuves,* had just been given to him for his story 'The Burial' by a jury made up of Andrée Chédid, Max-Pol Fouchet, Louis Martin-Chauffier, and Manès Sperber. This story would be published in April in an issue of *Preuves* edited by Jean Bloch-Michel." In *Jeune Afrique,* no. 274 (March 27, 1966): 41.

"*Asinus, Asnous,* and Ass" first appeared in *Les nouvelles littéraires* 2518 (February 5, 1976): 20–21.

"Saving the Fish" first appeared in *Les nouvelles littéraires* 2543 (July 29, 1976): 11.

"Of Djinns and Men" first appeared in *Les nouvelles littéraires* 2547 (August 26, 1976): 17.

"Returning to Morocco" was completed in Rabat on August 11, 1981, and first appeared in *Ruptures* 2 (1981): 13–14.

"The *Hashshashins*" was never published; instead, it was found typewritten among the author's papers with corrections made by hand. It was completed on March 9, 1986, in Mohammedia, when the author was staying with a friend, to whose daughter the text is dedicated.

"Elementary Word" first appeared in *Le message de la nation* 118 (March 29, 1986): 54, and was subsequently reprinted in *Esprit,* February 1991, 124–25.

"The Ghoul" first appeared in *Le Matin du Sahara Magazine,* March 16–23, 1986, 19, and was subsequently reprinted in *Esprit,* February 1991, 121–23.

"A Killer" first appeared in *Le message de la nation* 122 (April 22, 1986): 54.

"[In All Subjectivity]" was never published; instead, it was found handwritten on four sheets of paper torn from a notebook. It was likely intended for the German magazine *Merian;* Khaïr-Eddine addressed a letter to the magazine's editor, Rolf Hosfeld, on May 17, 1986, enclosing this piece.

"My Grandmother" first appeared in *Autrement* 48 (September 1990): 102–4.

"Trash" was completed in Rabat on September 24, 1993, and first appeared in *Le Matin du Sahara,* October 4, 1994, 4.

"Some Kind of Paris" was completed in Safir-Rabat on November 11, 1993, and first appeared in *Al Maghrib,* November 8, 1993, 6.

"Reptiles" was completed in Safir-Rabat on October 30, 1993, and first appeared in *Al Maghrib,* November 15, 1993, 6. It was subsequently reprinted in *Tifinagh* 3–4 (April–July 1994): 161–63.

"Catastrophes and Plagues" first appeared in *Jeune Afrique* 1717 (December 2–8, 1993): 81.

"Two Cutthroats" first appeared in *Al Asas* 118 (1994): 45–50.

"Two Cutthroats (2)" was completed in the National Institute for Oncology in Rabat in November 1993 and first appeared in *Al Asas* 119 (1994): 45–50.

"The Fisherman and the Ocean" was completed in Rabat on September 26, 1993, and first appeared in *Tidmi* 3 (October 27, 1994): 12.

"The Grandfather" first appeared in *Tidmi* 8 (December 27, 1994–January 2, 1995): 12.

"Cities" first appeared in *Tidmi* 12 (January 31–February 6, 1995): 12.

"The Argan Tree" was completed in Rabat on October 12, 1993, and first appeared in *Tidmi* 17 (March 28–April 3, 1995): 12.

"Two Ghouls" was written in Marrakech-Rabat between July and November 1994 and first appeared in *Esprit,* March–April 1995, 179–81.

"Seen from the Canopy" was completed in Rabat on September 29, 1993, and first appeared in *Tidmi* 26 (May 30–June 5, 1995): 12.

"The Asylum" was completed in Rabat on October 16, 1993, and first appeared in *Tidmi* 27 (June 6–12, 1995): 12.

"The House" was never published; instead, it was typewritten, signed, and dated in Rabat on October 9, 1994.

"The Last Will and Testament of a Dying Man" was completed in Rabat in February 1994 and first appeared in *Esprit,* January–February 1996, 28–35.

AFTERWORD

Teresa Villa-Ignacio

Readers of this collection of short prose pieces may already be familiar with Mohammed Khaïr-Eddine thanks to the handful of works now available in English, including his first poetry collection, *Scorpionic Sun (Soleil arachnide),* translated by Conor Bracken (Cleveland State University Poetry Center, 2019), and his first major novel/hybrid work *Agadir,* translated by Pierre Joris and Jake Syersak (Diálogos, 2020).[1] The devastating 1960 Agadir earthquake, which killed between twelve thousand and fifteen thousand of the city's residents and displaced tens of thousands more, figures prominently in both texts. In the novel, it is a physical reality that becomes an allegory for Moroccan decolonization. In what I have called the "seismic line" featured in "Black Nausea," *Scorpionic Sun*'s opening poem, it is an objective correlative for Moroccan identity in that tumultuous political moment.[2] In both texts, too, various creatures—including hyenas, jackals, and even humans—dig up buried bodies, and themes and motifs of unearthing, the grotesque, and disgust reign. Larbi Touaf views these overturnings of physical foundations in parallel to that of social foundations; that is, the "earthquake" of decolonization became the opportunity to rebuild the Moroccan nation from scratch.[3] Yet Khaïr-Eddine's texts beg the question: how can we rebuild when we can't trust the ground under our feet?

Khaïr-Eddine's personal trajectory reflects that of his seismic times. Born in 1941 in the southern Moroccan city of Tafraout, he spent his early childhood in the village of Azro Wado, and, as a member of the Indigenous Shilha people of the anti-Atlas, he spoke Tashlhiyt as his first language and learned French and Arabic in school. At eleven, he moved to Casablanca with his father after his parents' divorce; leaving his mother behind was traumatic for the young Khaïr-Eddine. A brilliant student, he published poems in his adolescence and sought like-minded company. In the early 1960s, he cowrote the influential manifesto *Poésie toute* with Mostafa Nissabouri and participated in the founding of the avant-garde Moroccan literary journal *Souffles,* where he published poems alongside those of other emerging great writers of his generation: Abdellatif Laâbi, Nissabouri, Tahar Ben Jelloun, and Abdelkébir Khatibi. However, Khaïr-Eddine had long had his sights set on Paris. He moved there in 1965 and worked briefly in factories, along with many other immigrant workers. His writings quickly vaulted him to critical acclaim, and he published short works frequently in reviews including *Esprit, Présence africaine, Les lettres nouvelles,* and *Les temps modernes.* He returned to Morocco in 1979 and lived there until his death in 1995. The author of more than thirty volumes of poetry, fiction, and nonfiction, he is best known for what he called his "linguistic guerrilla" tactics.[4] In life, these were matched by his outsize personality, which, though often exacerbated by alcoholism, was always beloved by his friends and readers. In a 1966 interview, Jamal Al Achgar characterizes Khaïr-Eddine's writing as a "permanent earthquake," with which the writer agrees: "A natural or fictional earthquake is always taking place. Always. It represents the structure of words, and therefore a world that isn't definitive, but always in perpetual fusion."[5] As this outlook suggests, Khaïr-Eddine embraced the poetics of precarity, riding out the shock waves toward innovative perspectives on humanity.

The Burial and Other Short Prose, 1963–1994, is not a book that existed in Khaïr-Eddine's lifetime. It was compiled after his death by the scholar Abdellatif Abboubi and published by Jean-Paul Michel, the editor of the Bordeaux-based press William Blake & Co., which has brought out revised editions of several of Khaïr-Eddine's works as well as some posthumous publications. The twenty-six texts in this volume range in length from one page to a dozen, and each in its own way articulates the author's poetics, ethics, and value system. Together, they showcase the diversity of his writing and its evolution over time. The texts were published in French and Moroccan reviews between 1966 and 1996, and the volume includes three texts that were never published while he was alive. Only the first four pieces date from before his return to Morocco, and in many ways the collection testifies to a more mature vision of his home country, one tempered by a long, self-imposed exile. Although Michel classifies the texts as "prose" and Bracken follows that classification, it's important to remember that the distinction between prose and poetry was never very important to Khaïr-Eddine: many of his poems are well and truly prose poems, and many of his "novels" include verse, drama, and other experimental forms.[6]

In view of Michel's categorization of these texts as "proses brèves" (brief works of prose), I'd like to suggest that they proleptically participate in what the writer Pierre Alferi (himself of Maghrebi, specifically Algerian Jewish, descent) calls the "bref" or "brief" genre emerging in the early twenty-first century as an effect of the digital technologies newly structuring our lives.[7] For Alferi, being brief doesn't just mean being short; it means expressing oneself within a particular kind of poetic economy, one that emphasizes irony and paradox, exemplifying the Latin virtue of *brevitas*.[8] While Khaïr-Eddine did not live to experience the internet and the proliferation of its brief genres, these texts exemplify their features and effects: their approaches to the ironies and paradoxes of human existence are elegant, humorous, and incisive by turns, and their condensed wisdom often cradles whole universes within their few pages.

Though these texts speak to universal human experiences, in writing them, Khaïr-Eddine was also interested in conveying his people's singularity. In elaborating the various facets of Shilha oral history gathered here—legends, daily life, reflections on social values and justice—he was participating in that tradition both by drawing on and disseminating traditional folklore and by inventing some of his own.[9] Stories such as "Of Djinns and Men" and "Two Ghouls" take for granted human coexistence with otherworldly spirits and creatures, such as the bogeywoman Tagmart Ismadal, who wreak their incomprehensible judgments on humans. Others suggest that there is no universal code of justice but rather that justice is determined one case at a time, depending on context, such as the need to avenge family members in "A Killer" and the tenuous but stable coexistence of a murderer and a Sufi in the same social space in "Reptiles." Within this worldview, it becomes difficult to adjudicate violations of the natural order of things when it's not clear whether humans or otherworldly beings are responsible, as in the case of the mysterious spirit-woman digging up the buried corpses of stillborn and young children in "The Ghoul." Neither witch hunts nor the colonial authorities can put a stop to the horrors, which end abruptly when a middle-aged woman's home goes up in flames: "And that was it." While all the villagers seem to accept this explanation, readers may be unsatisfied or, at least, may wonder whether there is more to the story than the recounting of an extraordinary occurrence. First published in 1986, "The Ghoul" recalls Khaïr-Eddine's 1973 novel *Le déterreur* (The unearther), whose first-person male narrator digs up corpses and eats them. In an interview, Khaïr-Eddine explained that there was a real "unearther" in southern Morocco on whom the novel is based and from whom he took the idea that the writer must unearth "what is most sacred in society, make the public aware of it, and criticize it."[10] Taking "unearthing" as his guiding approach to writing is a testament to Khaïr-Eddine's commitment to utter radicalism in literature.

It is no coincidence that Khaïr-Eddine sought guidance from Shilha oral history when advocating for the full acknowledgment of Amazigh identity in the Moroccan public sphere. A grassroots movement to publicly highlight and prioritize Amazigh language and culture has been active in Morocco since the 1960s, and it comprises hundreds of organizations focused variously on cultural action, the arts, history, and language advocacy. Khaïr-Eddine is considered a leading figure in what Brahim El Guabli calls "Morocco's re-Amazighation" and is revered for contributing to an Amazigh-centered "alternative memory in lieu of or parallel to the Arab-Islamic-centered official history."[11] Tamazight, of which Khaïr-Eddine's native Tashlhiyt is a dialect, is spoken by about 45 percent of Moroccans, and the movement toward its standardization has resulted in the use of the Amazigh Tifinagh alphabet in all public areas, along with Arabic and French.[12] Khaïr-Eddine directly addresses the complexities of standardizing and technologically disseminating Tamazight in the posthumous novel *Il était une fois un vieux couple heureux* (2002; Once upon a time, there was a happy old couple). In the book, which Khaïr-Eddine completed in 1993, the protagonist, Bouchaib, writes an epic poem in Tamazight. His imam wants to print it and distribute it on the radio and on videocassette, which Bouchaib fears may amount to uprooting and commodifying his local culture. In Erin Twohig's view, Khaïr-Eddine questions whether writing and technological reproduction are suitable modes of preservation for oral culture and, through this "seemingly innocuous narrative," condemns the dangers of "folklorization."[13]

Yet Khaïr-Eddine also emphasizes that oral culture is neither static nor frozen in some inaccessible, eternal past. It changes as the times change and incorporates modernity,[14] as in the beating heart of this collection, the two-part "Two Cutthroats," an extended parable of colonial subjectivity first published in 1994. Its protagonist, The Killer, and his sidekick, The Butcher, have had their identities subsumed under their social functions; relying only on their "reptilian brain," these unreflective powermongers use violence remorselessly as a means to their ends. Yet we are liable to sympathize with The Killer and The Butcher, perhaps because Khaïr-Eddine's descriptions of them are so entertaining, or perhaps because they are the heroes of the story and the narrative structure compels us to desire their success. At the end of the story, when The Killer is so easily converted to a colonial functionary, we see how colonizers literally employed immoral criminals to get the work of colonizing done, taking advantage of their complicity and their violent role within the existing social order. Any ambivalence readers may have felt about The Killer may be either resolved or deepened once he becomes a member of the colonial apparatus. This ambivalence is the colonial experience *par excellence*. Khaïr-Eddine shows us how colonizing narratives teach us to love and fear those who ultimately do us in: luring us in, and catching us in our questionable allegiances, is a guiding feature of his linguistic guerrilla warfare.

The Killer's absolute complicity is, of course, not the only effect of colonialism on subjectivity in Khaïr-Eddine's repertoire. "The Asylum" introduces us to neocolonial subjects with limited agency in the form of abandoned psychiatric patients, most of whose lives were ruined by the western introduction of LSD to the Essaourian peninsula. The final story of the collection, "The

Last Will and Testament of a Dying Man," written when Khaïr-Eddine himself was close to death, features an evolving postcolonial subject, a cantankerous, democratic head of state whose deathbed critiques of his immediate successors' incompetencies belie the faith that his people will choose democracy in the end. Many of the texts in the collection testify to a colonial society that in some ways was more inclusive than the one that followed it. "Two Cutthroats" describes wanderers from the south accepted as "brothers" by the villagers and Jewish characters of all kinds living among the Amazigh, including the Jewish loan shark whose treasure The Killer helps himself to and whose daughter he rapes; Mardukh, the Jewish saddlemaker turned *mahia* sommelier; the Jews in Talbordjt, the Agadir medina "where Jews and Muslims lived side by side"; and the Jewish arms dealer nephew of the loan shark in Agadir, whose loyalty The Killer gains by declaring, apparently sincerely, "'Jews are men just like any other. . . . Whoever injures or persecutes them ought to be severely punished, because they are people of the Book, just like Christians and Muslims.'"[15] Perhaps the most important colonial subject here is the people as a collective, which often serves as a kind of Greek chorus in these stories, much as in some of Khaïr-Eddine's dramatic texts. "Two Cutthroats" describes our ambivalence about living in society: "Those nights, you could feel the complete fragility of the human condition, as well as a strange sympathy for one's fellow man tangled up with dread and repressed tenderness, because it is hard to think of oneself as anything significant in the face of the fathomless infinity in which each being, each elementary particle, nevertheless had its own place of honor." This passage, which ends a long description of the tradition of welcoming strangers into the community with a village feast, emblematizes the ambivalence of collective subjectivity, even beyond the colonial condition, within Khaïr-Eddine's expansive vision of human complexity.

Khaïr-Eddine was deeply invested in exploring how political repression transforms subjectivity and how subjectivity must transform itself to survive violations of individual and collective self-determination. A French protectorate from 1912 to 1956, Morocco's immediate postcolonial condition was structured by Hassan II's authoritarian regime, known as the Years of Lead, a period of repression from the 1960s to the 1980s that involved disappearances, torture, and execution of dissidents; for those who were allowed to live in society, it was a period of silence and fear of reprisals.[16] As Khalid Lyamlahy observes, Khaïr-Eddine sought, throughout his life and in his writing, a "sovereign subjectivity" made manifest by his self-exile to France and explicit denunciation of the authoritarian regime during that period.[17] Many features of his early work establish him as an innovative resister of hegemonic power, one who puts the sacrosanct, whole, embodied subject in question, takes violations of embodied human subjectivity to their very limits, and then pushes further.

Over the course of his life and œuvre, however, we witness Khaïr-Eddine shift his focus from unearthing to living on Earth, to what Lyamlahy identifies as a "dynamics of introspection and self-reconstruction" as an alternative to hegemonic sovereignty.[18] Central to this introspection and self-reconstruction is Khaïr-Eddine's valorization of participation in place. "Returning to Morocco," written two years after his return, celebrates his reconnection with the "spotless solitudes" and the "turbulent shading characteristic of the world's beginning" essential to his work, and it describes his engagement in the ongoing collective struggles for self-respect through respect for the land and against the co-optation of culture as folklorism for tourist consumption. In "*Asinus, Asnous,* and Ass," Khaïr-Eddine reveals that his use of the French language is a product of his upbringing in a multilingual homeland. Rejecting the opposition to French due to its colonial legacy as a narrow-minded approach to the language, he describes his appreciation of its beauty, history, and ability to connect him with other writers of French expression. Khaïr-Eddine's placefulness is not limited to Morocco, however. "Some Kind of Paris" paints famous landmarks with reverence and irreverence in equal measure: the Place de la Contrescarpe becomes a makeshift dormitory for drunkards, and the banks of the Seine a hot spot for intrepid fishermen; for a village-dweller like Khaïr-Eddine, Paris is a village like any other. And "Cities" praises ancient cities, from Troy to Essaouira, for avoiding the frenzy of modernity and supplying material for poetry.

Khaïr-Eddine does not keep secret the fact that his writing draws on his personal, subjective experience. However, as he indicates in the piece "[In All Subjectivity]," he introduces auto-biographical content on his own terms: "Nothing's really been new since the world was created. Except the shading, yes, that—the grayish-white turning gradually to black where colors woven into the unabridged blue of an incandescent eternity cross over one another. I won't say my name a single time, though. I will describe my life and I'll describe it just as an entomologist describes a beetle or how a zoologist describes a mammal and its phylogenesis." These analogies, reminiscent of Émile Zola's naturalism, suggest that for Khaïr-Eddine, the endpoint of the scientific study of his own life—and, implicitly, any and all other lives—is literary. He also returns to the motif of writing as "shading," giving dimension to factuality. This shading is exquisite in the eponymous opening piece, "The Burial," which reads like an early chapter of a memoir. The child learns of the fact of death through an experience of social rites that are not so much explained as painfully lived, yet the child's perception of himself as disruptive creates tension with a narratorial vision of the child's disruptions as part of the social flow. Khaïr-Eddine's life also enters into the texts of this volume through several dedications to his Moroccan friends, including the scientists and doctors Mehdi El Mandjra, Brahim Gueddari, and Methqal; the politicians Moulay Driss Aloui Ismaïli, Hassan Abouyoub, and Zohour Alaoui, who was the Moroccan ambassador to Sweden and UNESCO; and the French writer and editor Denis Roche, whose 1972 manifesto *La poésie est inadmissible* (Poetry is unacceptable) Khaïr-Eddine surely read as a tantalizing challenge.

Perhaps the most moving autobiographical moment is Khaïr-Eddine's tribute to his grandmother and mother, which praises women's role in transmitting Amazigh knowledge of the natural world as both cultural heritage and a necessity for safeguarding the environment in the present and future. Throughout his œuvre, Khaïr-Eddine engages this heritage and necessity by foregrounding every possible element of the natural landscape, from flora and fauna to mountains and deserts. The diverse, environmentally oriented pieces collected here directly praise nature and express concern about human abuses of the environment. They

range from the stories that reveal his passion for fishing (and ex-
hort the reader not to pollute the sea) to his prose poem in praise
of the argan tree's hardiness and longevity and to the nasty ver-
sion of the sublime in "Trash" that nevertheless marvels at the
birds and insects that persist in creating ecosystems within garbage dumps. Khaïr-Eddine's fascination with all branches of science extends outward from our planetary environment to the
cosmos, as in "Elementary Word," a monologue from the point
of view of a haughty hydrogen atom that remembers the Big
Bang. At the same time, he portrays alternate worlds with technical virtuosity in stories like "The *Hashshashins*," a surreal,
dreamlike adventure, and "The House," a dream of his ancestral
home turned into a labyrinth.

Khaïr-Eddine's technical virtuosity is a quality we have come
to expect from the great Francophone Moroccan writers of his
generation, who, like him, were all politically engaged intel-
lectuals and all eventually settled in France or split their time
between France and Morocco. Tahar Ben Jelloun (b. 1947), a
psychiatrist by training, has brought novels, essays, and poetry
to bear on the experiences of immigrants and political prisoners
and is known for his critiques of Islamophobia and terrorism.
Abdellatif Laâbi's (b. 1942) writing ranges from avant-garde
political poetry to realist novels and essays dedicated to human-
ism in all its forms. The works of Abdelkébir Khatibi (1938–
2009), a sociologist by training, delve into unexpected histories
of tattoos, calligraphy, Islamic mysticism, and more; he is also
the author of important works of Maghrebi literary criticism.
Khaïr-Eddine distinguished himself among them with his extreme avant-gardism and his commitment to making his Indigenous identity visible, even after he returned to Morocco and
perhaps adopted a more indirect approach to political critique
than his contemporaries living in France did. This generation
of decolonial writers introduced the complexity of contemporary Morocco to the world, forcing us to move beyond western
clichés about Morocco and Francophone North Africa perpe-
trated by the popular media.[19]

In a tribute published in *Le Monde* upon Khaïr-Eddine's
death, Ben Jelloun ranked him with the Algerian Kateb Yacine
and the Martinican Aimé Césaire as the three writers who have

most "overturned and enriched" the French language.[20] Khaïr-Eddine indeed acknowledged the importance of innovating within the French language as a motivation for his writing. In a 1979 interview with the Mauritian poet Édouard Maunick, Khaïr-Eddine identified with a range of Francophone writers: Césaire, the Irish Samuel Beckett, the Senegalese Léopold Sédar Senghor, and the Belgian Henri Michaux were "bringing a new language to France," not in an extractive way that recalls colonialism but in introducing a diversity of "linguistic genius" and "evocative power" to the language.[21] This drive to innovate the French language makes possible the greatness, and often epic quality, of Khaïr-Eddine's works.

It is not out of the question that we should read Khaïr-Eddine's œuvre as an epic vision of modern-day Morocco, emerging from millennia of tradition and the decades of colonialism that threw it all into question. Recent translations by Jake Syersak affirm this commitment to historicizing, reconciling, and envisioning the complex imagined community that is Morocco. *I, Caustic* (2022; *Moi l'aigre,* 1970), which mixes prose, drama, free verse, and diatribe, portrays a Moroccan pre-apocalypse in which overthrowing the hegemonic sovereign appears vertiginously possible and absurd. The two poetry collections take up similar themes. *Proximal Morocco—*(2023; *Ce Maroc!,* 1975) spells out, in lavish Khaïr-Eddinian fashion, every last natural, historical, and sociocultural detail of his beloved "Sudique" region, while *Resurrection of Wildflowers* (2022; *Résurrection des fleurs sauvages,* 1981/1994) celebrates Khaïr-Eddine's return to his native land while expanding the reach of his poetic wonder to a global scale. Bracken observes that "his work feels part of a larger, international conversation that includes poets like Raúl Zurita, Kim Hyesoon, Joyelle McSweeney, and others, who approach poetry as an almost hallucinatory, but also politically engaged, practice."[22] Within a longer tradition of hallucinatory poetics, Khaïr-Eddine is so often compared to Arthur Rimbaud not only because of the rapprochement of their poetic sensibilities and will to overthrow authoritarianism but also because we need Khaïr-Eddine in the same way we need Rimbaud: as a poet who deregulates all our senses, changes our ideas about what poetry can do, and makes it impossible for us to ignore our fragile, material, embodied existences on our fragile planet. For Khaïr-Eddine, political, personal, and planetary concerns continuously erupt together as a churning mass of ecstatic chaos whose occasional forays into order must be critically questioned lest they tip over into oppression.

This poetic complexity is not only overwhelming to read but also particularly challenging to translate. Khaïr-Eddine's pluri-disciplinary erudition flares not only in his vast subject matter but in his use of many French words of regional origin, such as *engeance* for "race," which arrived circuitously via Limousin or Sardinian from the Latin, or *goéland,* Breton for "gull," a type of bird. Such moves indicate his solidarity with the heritage speakers of France's minoritized languages. His texts are also teeming with Arabic and Tamazight words: *fquih, deofels,* and *jnouns* populate his tales, while his mother's *haïk,* many fes-tive *moussems,* and the blistering *chergui* make appearances. As Syersak observes, "Khaïr-Eddine is using the words from his Moroccan homeland to foster a feeling of alienation and oth-erness in the reader—the same feelings he had as an exile. He wants them to wade knee deep in it, twist and turn through its muck, and confront it."[23] Throughout the collection, Bracken carefully chooses how to render the text's multilingualism, pri-oritizing a polyphony of sound, flow, and rhythm that master-fully wrestles Khaïr-Eddine's lengthy, complex sentences into an intensely enjoyable English.

What's more, Bracken deftly captures the singular mix of genius and irreverence, the over-the-top hyperbole so eloquent that we take it seriously, that characterizes Khaïr-Eddine's writ-ing, as in this simultaneous praise and condemnation of Hassan Ibn Al-Sabbah, the leader of the legendary medieval Order of Assassins:

Your laws, pronounced in the sumptuous silence of the mountains, among the very rocks where scuffled the beasts they said were our ancestors, your laws and your incantation set to the rhythms of central rays of quasars fascinated everyone who had never read a thing; you enchanted us; our bodies were floating in the galactic denial of cannabis—the oceans, heavy with their wonders, sand, and rocks jutting out of time's deepest wrinkle unfurled beneath our eyes as soon as you began to speak; this is how you smoke-screened the universe . . .

Spanning high and low registers and standard and dialectical French within a sentence is a Khaïr-Eddinian ability that carries over beautifully in Bracken's American English, richly informed by all other Englishes. He matches the original's never-ending torrent of humor, irony, and idiomatic expressions, giving us characters who have "bats in the belfry" or are "totally rung" or "washed up," another who's a "tough nut to crack," and yet another who emphasizes his absolute faith in prayer with that unforgettable expression immortalized in the musical *Annie,* "bet your bottom dollar"! This collection in particular presents additional challenges with its range of styles, diversity of characters' voices, and most of all its thirty-year span of the author's work and life. Bracken meets all Khaïr-Eddinian translation challenges with aplomb—unsurprisingly, as he first wowed us with the explosive power of *Scorpionic Sun* and has examined in his own poetry, with terrifying intimacy, such unforgiving realities as America's ongoing complicity in Henry Kissinger's legacy of neocolonial sovereignty.[24] Bracken may have taken as his own poetic and translational motto a line from another of his translatees, the Haitian Jean D'Amérique: "I aim for the language of rage's lanes."[25]

In the ongoing, enthusiastic Anglosphere reception of Khaïr-Eddine, the current volume will serve as a bridge between his earlier works and, hopefully, forthcoming translations of more prose works, including *Légende et vie d'Agoun'chich, Le déterreur,* and *Il était une fois un vieux couple heureux.* This volume affords us an at once luxurious and necessary window into the complex diversity of Morocco and the Maghreb, or, as the Amazigh have called it for thousands of years, Tamzagha. Like the hospitable villagers in so many of his tales, Mohammed Khaïr-Eddine has invited us outsiders to partake in a feast, and afterward, we may, like them, be good for nothing but to look up into the night sky and contemplate the wonder of it all.

Notes

1. Seuil published *Soleil arachnide* in 1969; a new edition in 2009 by Jean-Paul Michel follows the order of the book's composition and is the basis of Bracken's translation. *Agadir* was first published by Seuil in 1967.
2. Teresa Villa-Ignacio, "Postcolonial Disgust and Poetic Responsibility in Mohammed Khaïr-Eddine's *Nausée Noire,*" *Yale French Studies* 137/138 (2020): 175.
3. Larbi Touaf, "The Legacy of Dissent: Mohamed Khair-Eddine and the Ongoing Cultural Diversity Debate in Morocco," *Journal of North African Studies* 21, no. 1 (2016): 156–61.
4. Mohammed Khaïr-Eddine, *Moi l'aigre* (Paris: Seuil, 1970), 28. Unless otherwise noted, all translations are my own. See Abdellatif Abboubi, *Bibliographie de Mohammed Khaïr-Eddine 1962–2014* (Paris: L'Harmattan, 2023), for a prodigious list of Khaïr-Eddine's texts as well as a list of critical works on his œuvre.
5. Mohammed Khaïr-Eddine, *Le temps des refus: Entretiens 1966–1995,* ed. Abdellatif Abboubi (Paris: L'Harmattan, 1998), 15.
6. Conor Bracken and Jake Syersak, "On Translating Mohammed Khaïr-Eddine," interview by Khalid Lyamlahy, *Asymptote,* September 7, 2023.
7. Pierre Alferi, *Brefs* (Paris: P. O. L., 2016), 157–58.
8. Alferi, *Brefs,* 159, 162.
9. To get a sense of this tradition, readers of French may peruse the colonial linguist Émile Laoust's transcribed, translated, and annotated collection of Tashlhiyt folktales, collected between 1913 and 1920 near Marrakesh, in *Contes berbères du Maroc: Textes berbères du groupe Beraber-Chleuh (Maroc Central, Haut, et Anti-Atlas). Traduits et annotés,* Publications de l'Institut des Hautes Études Marocains 1 (Paris: Éditions Larose, 1949).
10. Khaïr-Eddine, *Temps des refus,* 41–42.
11. Brahim El Guabli, *Moroccan Other-Archives: History and Citizenship After State Violence* (New York: Fordham University Press, 2023), 36; see also 212n44. Thomas Connolly adopts Khaïr-Eddine's phrase "secret music" to describe the Chleuh rhythms in his poetry and prose (see *A Poetic Genealogy of North African Literature* [Evanston, IL: Northwestern University Press, 2025], 87), and Touaf argues that Khaïr-Eddine's writing demonstrates how

contemporary Amazigh activism constitutes a Hughesian "dream deferred" from the 1960s and 1970s ("Legacy of Dissent," 52).

12. El Guabli, *Moroccan Other-Archives,* 28–31.

13. Erin Twohig, "Literature and Amazigh Language Debates: The Case of Moroccan Amazigh Literature in 'Other' Languages," *Journal of North African Studies* 22, no. 4 (2017): 548–50.

14. See Paulette Galand-Pernet's *Recueil de poèmes chleuhs; chants des trouveurs* (Paris: Klincksieck, 1972) for a transcription, French translation, and careful annotation of Tashlhiyt poems collected in the 1950s and 1960s, contemporary with the beginning of Khaïr-Eddine's career. Some of these poems feature timely subjects, including the experiences of migrant laborers in France and Algeria.

15. See El Guabli, *Moroccan Other-Archives,* 5–6, on the tandem marginalization of the Moroccan Amazigh and Jewish peoples during the Years of Lead, and chaps. 2–3 on efforts to preserve and deepen the collective memory of the Morocco shared by Jews and Muslims before the post–World War II Jewish exodus.

16. See Christine Daure-Serfaty, *Tazmamart: Une prison de la mort au Maroc* (Paris: Stock, 1992); Ahmed Marzouki, *Tazmamart: Cellule 10* (Paris: Gallimard, 2001); Susan Slyomovics, *The Performance of Human Rights in Morocco* (Philadelphia: University of Pennsylvania Press, 2005); Zakya Daoud, *Maroc: Les années de plomb, 1958–1988: Chroniques d'une résistance* (Houilles, France: Éditions Mancius, 2007); and El Guabli, *Moroccan Other-Archives,* chap. 4.

17. Khalid Lyamlahy, "Toward an Aesthetics of Self-Sovereignty: The Symbolic of Anti-Authoritarian Discourse in Mohammed Khaïr-Eddine's *Agadir,*" *Research in African Literatures* 49, no. 3 (2018): 135.

18. Lyamlahy, "Aesthetics of Self-Sovereignty," 148.

19. See Brian T. Edwards, *Morocco Bound: Disorienting America's Maghreb, from Casablanca to the Marrakesh Express* (Durham, NC: Duke University Press, 2005), for a history and problematization of this tendency.

20. Tahar Ben Jelloun, "Khair-Eddine ou la fureur de dire," *Le Monde. fr,* December 1, 1995.

21. Khaïr-Eddine, *Temps des refus,* 59.

22. Bracken and Syersak, "On Translating."

23. Bracken and Syersak, "On Translating."

24. Conor Bracken, *The Enemy of My Enemy Is Me* (Doha, Qatar, and Richmond, VA: Diode Editions, 2021), 29–38.

25. Jean D'Amérique, *No Way in the Skin Without This Bloody Embrace,* trans. Conor Bracken (Brooklyn: Ugly Duckling Presse, 2022), 29.

GLOSSARY

Asterisk indicates note supplied by Khaïr-Eddine in the original.

acridian	Of or relating to the order of orthopterous insects, which includes locusts and grasshoppers
Adrar	Tamazight for "mountain"*
aerolite	Stony meteorite
Al Asnam	The town of Chlef, capital of the eponymous province in Algeria, which was struck by a magnitude 7.1 earthquake in 1980, causing massive damage, displacement, and death; not to be confused with *The Book of Idols*, a work by Hisham ibn al-Kalbi which discusses religion in pre-Islamic Arabia
Amghar	Regional authority of the old South*
Ammelns	A valley in the Anti-Atlas mountains
cadi	An Islamic judge*
caïdat	A unit of Moroccan administrative organization akin to a district, larger than a village or rural commune but smaller than a prefecture
caïd	The administrator of a caïdat, and an important component of the Makhzen
chergui	An easterly wind out of the Sahara
Colonel Justinard	Léopold Justinard (1878–1959), aka Capitaine Chleuh, a French military officer who served in the colonial military and administration in Algeria and, more consequentially, in Morocco
cope	A cape worn by Catholic and Anglican priests, often richly embroidered; also known as a pluviale
datura	Any of nine species of poisonous flowering plants belonging to the nightshade family;

	known commonly as jimsonweeds, mad apples, or devil's trumpets
deofels	Alternate spelling of "devils"
djin	A shapeshifting spirit that may offer protection or cause harm
fquihs	Supernatural healers
gandoura	A light, short-sleeved, ankle-length tunic for both indoor and outdoor wear
guembri	A three-stringed bass lute used by the Gnawa people
gurglet	A porous earthen jar for cooling water via evaporation
haïk	A large piece of fabric that envelops the body head to toe as protection against the elements and as an expression of modesty
Haratins	A North African ethnic group distinct from Arab and Berber ethnic groups, historically marginalized due to their Blackness and economic and political discrimination
Hashshashins	Members of an order, founded by Hasan Al-Sabbah in 1090 CE, who killed perceived enemies of the Nizari Isma'ili state
House of Illigh	The physical headquarters of Ali Abou Hassan As-Semlali, ruler of the Souss region in southern Morocco in the seventeenth century
Ilbis	The leader of the devils in Islam; also known as Sheitan
jnouns	Djinns; an embodiment of the natural world's strength and capriciousness
kif	A traditional mixture of tobacco and cannabis; from the Arabic for "to enjoy"
koummya	A Moroccan term for a dagger; similar to a yatagan*
lotar	A Berber version of the *guembri*
maâlem	A master artisan of traditional Moroccan arts, such as tiling, metalwork, ceramics, and more, capable of and expected to instruct apprentices
mahia	A brandy made by Moroccan Jews from figs*

Makhzen	The royal military, which collaborated with the French colonial military
Marshal Lyautey	The Resident General of Morocco from 1912 to 1916 and 1917 to 1925 who, among other things, was in charge of pacifying restive areas of the protectorate
mechoui	Spit-roasted whole lamb or sheep
moghazni or Mokhzani	A service member of the royal military
moussems	Annual gatherings of tribes that facilitate economic, cultural, and social exchange
roumi	A non-Muslim; from the Arabic for "roman," normally used disparagingly
Seïba	A reference to the Bled es-Siba, regions of Morocco that were not directly under the control of the Sultan (unlike the Bled el-Makhzen); often inhabited by Berber tribes; from the Arabic for "rebellion" or "anarchy"
Sherifian Empire	The name used to refer to the political entity of Morocco, current from the sixteenth to the twentieth centuries
Souss	A region in southern Morocco important in trans-Saharan trade and capital of the Chleuh Amazigh ethnic group
Supervielle	Jules Supervielle (1884–1960), Franco-Uruguayan poet and writer
trionyxes	African softshell turtles
Zanuck	Darryl F. Zanuck (1902–1979), an American film producer and studio executive; one of the founders of 20th Century Fox

BIBLIOGRAPHY

Abboubi, Abdellatif. *Bibliographie de Mohammed Khaïr-Eddine 1962–2014*. Paris: L'Harmattan, 2023.

Alferi, Pierre. *Brefs*. Paris: P. O. L., 2016.

Ben Jelloun, Tahar. "Khair-Eddine ou la fureur de dire." *Le Monde.fr*, December 1, 1995.

Bracken, Conor. *The Enemy of My Enemy Is Me*. Doha, Qatar, and Richmond, VA: Diode Editions, 2021.

Bracken, Conor, and Jake Syersak. "On Translating Mohammed Khaïr-Eddine." Interview by Khalid Lyamlahy. *Asymptote*, September 7, 2023.

Connolly, Thomas. *A Poetic Genealogy of North African Literature*. Evanston, IL: Northwestern University Press, 2025.

D'Amérique, Jean. *No Way in the Skin Without This Bloody Embrace*. Translated by Conor Bracken. Brooklyn: Ugly Duckling Presse, 2022.

Daoud, Zakya. *Maroc: Les années de plomb, 1958–1988: Chroniques d'une résistance*. Houilles, France: Éditions Mancius, 2007.

Daure-Serfaty, Christine. *Tazmamart: Une prison de la mort au Maroc*. Paris: Stock, 1992.

Edwards, Brian T. *Morocco Bound: Disorienting America's Maghreb, from Casablanca to the Marrakesh Express*. Durham, NC: Duke University Press, 2005.

El Guabli, Brahim. *Moroccan Other-Archives: History and Citizenship After State Violence*. New York: Fordham University Press, 2023.

Ez-Zouaine, Younès. "Le paysage méditerranéen dans la poésie de Mohammed Khair-Eddine." *Babel: Littératures plurielles* 30 (2014): 199–216.

Galand-Pernet, Paulette. *Recueil de poèmes chleuhs; chants des trouveurs*. Paris: Klincksieck, 1972.

Gontard, Marc. *La violence du texte: La littérature marocaine de langue française*. Paris: L'Harmattan; Rabat: Société marocaine des éditeurs réunis, 1981.

———. "La violence du texte selon Khaïr-Eddine: L'exemple du *Déterreur*." *Expressions maghrébines* 5, no. 2 (2006): 5–16.

Khaïr-Eddine, Mohammed. *Agadir*. Paris: Seuil, 1967.

———. *Agadir*. Translated by Pierre Joris and Jake Syersak. New Orleans: Diálogos, 2020.

———. *Ce Maroc!* Paris: Seuil, 1975.

———. *I, Caustic.* Translated by Jake Syersak. New York: Litmus, 2022.

———. *Moi l'aigre.* Paris: Seuil, 1970.

———. *Résurrection des fleurs sauvages.* Rabat: Éditions Stouky, 1981.

———. *Resurrection of Wildflowers.* Translated by Jake Syersak. Buenos Aires and Rome: Oomph! Press, 2022.

———. *Scorpionic Sun.* Translated by Conor Bracken. Cleveland: Cleveland State University Poetry Center, 2019.

———. *Soleil arachnide.* Edited by Jean-Paul Michel. Paris: Gallimard, 1969.

———. *Le temps des refus: Entretiens 1966–1995.* Edited by Abdellatif Abboubi. Paris: L'Harmattan, 1998.

Laoust, Émile. *Contes berbères du Maroc: Textes berbères du groupe Beraber-Chleuh (Maroc Central, Haut, et Anti-Atlas). Traduits et annotés.* Publications de l'Institut des Hautes Études Marocains 1. Paris: Éditions Larose, 1949.

Lyamlahy, Khalid. "Moving Beyond Mobility: The Aesthetics of Exile and Becoming in Mohammed Khaïr-Eddine's 'Légende et Vie d'Agoun'chich.'" *Journal of North African Studies* 22, no. 2 (2017): 259–82.

———. *Nostalgic Rebels: Politics, Aesthetics, and Selfhood in Postcolonial Morocco.* Liverpool: Liverpool University Press, 2025.

———. "Le poète et sa 'vieille marotte calamiteuse': Figures et variations du grotesque dans la poésie de Mohammed Khaïr-Eddine." *International Journal of Francophone Studies* 20 (2020): 14–47.

———. "Toward an Aesthetics of Self-Sovereignty: The Symbolic of Anti-Authoritarian Discourse in Mohammed Khaïr-Eddine's *Agadir.*" *Research in African Literatures* 49, no. 3 (2018): 131–52.

Marzouki, Ahmed. *Tazmamart: Cellule 10.* Paris: Gallimard, 2001.

Rogers, Lynne D. "Mohammed Khaïr-Eddine's *Le Déterreur:* An Invitation to the Primal Repast." *Dalhousie French Studies* 30 (Spring 1995): 159–70.

Slyomovics, Susan. *The Performance of Human Rights in Morocco.* Philadelphia: University of Pennsylvania Press, 2005.

Touaf, Larbi. "The Legacy of Dissent: Mohamed Khair-Eddine and the Ongoing Cultural Diversity Debate in Morocco." *Journal of North African Studies* 21, no. 1 (2016): 50–59.

———. "The Sense and Non-Sense of Cultural Identity in Mohammed Khaïr-Eddine's Fiction." *Alif: Journal of Contemporary Poetics* 32 (2012): 151–66.

Twohig, Erin. "Literature and Amazigh Language Debates: The Case of Moroccan Amazigh Literature in 'Other' Languages." *Journal of North African Studies* 22, no. 4 (2017): 536–59.

Villa-Ignacio, Teresa. "Postcolonial Disgust and Poetic Responsibility in Mohammed Khaïr-Eddine's *Nausée Noire.*" *Yale French Studies* 137/138 (2020): 171–89.